VOICES OF THE SOUTH

Poor Fool

Other Books by
ERSKINE CALDWELL

POOR FOOL

ERSKINE CALDWELL

LOUISIANA STATE UNIVERSITY PRESS

Baton Rouge
and London

Designer: Glynnis Phoebe
Typeface: Text Bodoni, display Concept One
Typesetter: G & S Typesetters, Inc.
Printer and binder: Thomson-Shore, Inc.

Library of Congress Cataloging-in-Publication Data
Caldwell, Erskine, 1903–
   Poor fool / Erskine Caldwell.
      p.   cm.
   ISBN 0-8071-1947-4 (pbk.)
   I. Title.
PS3505.A322P6   1994
813′.52—dc20   94-11456
                                         CIP

The paper in this book meets the guidelines for permanence and durability of the
Committee on Production Guidelines for Book Longevity of the Council on Library
Resources. ∞

PART ONE
LOUISE

1

Blondy Niles sat hunched over the table in the cafe spitting in his coffee cup. Blondy was alone. The other tables in the place were crowded with bulb-eyed men and their lean clinging women. The electric piano slammed out a piece of jazz that everybody liked. A dark haired girl sitting at a table against the wall looked over the heads of the crowd at Blondy. A man sitting beside her put his arms around her neck and tried to unbutton her dress. She pushed him away. It was a little after midnight.

When Blondy stopped eating he shoved the dirty dishes to the other end of the table. He kept the coffee cup to spit in. At eleven o'clock he came in and ordered fried oysters. He had been eating potato salad and cold frankfurters for the past two weeks and he wanted something different. Salad and frankfurters cost twenty-five cents, fried oysters thirty-five. Chickory coffee was always a nickel.

The man who ran the cafe came in from a back room and looked the crowd over. Kroot was big and hairy and everytime he took a step his stride was a full yard. To run the cafe he had to be tough.

Before he saw Blondy one of the waiters pointed him out and told Kroot about Blondy spitting in the coffee mugs. The waiters were little men. They were afraid to say anything to a man like Blondy.

Kroot threw aside his cigar and pushed through the crowd to the table where Blondy sat. He was not afraid of anybody.

He spat the bitter taste of the cigar on the floor.

"What you doing here?"

He shoved Blondy upright in the chair with a slap of his hand. Kroot was over six feet tall and weighed close to two hundred and fifty. He ran a saloon before he opened the cafe and before that he had lifted weights in a circus.

"Who wants to know?" Blondy asked him.

"I'm the one what's going to know pretty damn quick," he said giving Blondy another shove with his big hand.

"Aw go to hell."

"Say. If you can't spit on the floor like the rest of us," he moved closer, "you'll have to get out. You can't stay here and spit in the mugs like that."

"Who's going to stop me?"

"Hey Bill! Come here!" he shouted to somebody in the back room. "Come here and bring the old man with you."

The "old man" was a lead pipe with the ends rounded smoothly. The pipe was rounded so the sharp edges would not break the scalp and make a lot of blood for the police to kick about.

The crowd turned around watching Blondy and Kroot and waiting for something to happen. The piano finished the piece it was playing. The dark slender girl who had been looking at Blondy stood on her chair to see what was happening. Kroot hitched up his pants.

The crowd waited for something to happen. That was what it was here for.

Blondy spat in the mug again and tossed it across the table. It hit the stack of dirty dishes and everything crashed to the floor making a big noise. Kroot kicked over the table and jerked Blondy off the chair to the floor. Just then the man came running in from the back room and whacked Blondy over the head several times with the pipe. Kroot snatched the pipe from the other's hand and gave Blondy a couple more on the head. Blondy stood on his feet. The man whacked him again with the pipe and stood back for him to fall. Blondy stood on his feet like a cast-iron horse in a blacksmith's shop. The crowd was hoping to see a good fight but Blondy stood motionless. He once hit a man in the ring so hard he cleared the top rope by four inches. He had been a killer in those days.

Kroot hit him another half dozen times as fast as he could draw back the pipe. Blondy fell over against the table knocked out cold. The crowd turned around and the electric piano started all over again.

"All right Bill," Kroot said to the other. "Dump him out."

The man grabbed Blondy by his feet and dragged him to the door and rolled him out. Some men coming up the street kicked him out of the way into the gutter.

2

When Blondy opened his eyes he was propped against the cafe wall in the alley and the slender girl who had looked at him across the tables was on her knees beside him.

"How do you feel?" she asked.

Blondy looked at her and said nothing. His head felt a mile away and it was sore like a wound tonight. He did not feel like talking to her.

"What made you keep on spitting in the cup like that?" she asked insistently.

Blondy had never seen the girl before to have anything to do with her. His head was feeling further and further away.

She kept on asking him questions.

"What's it to you?"

"I hated to see you get beat up like that."

"Well what's it to you? You don't belong to me."

"It wouldn't have happened if you had stopped when he told you. You didn't have to keep it up."

Blondy ignored the girl and searched for a match and cigarette. The girl bothered him. He wanted to be left alone.

"Why did you do it?" she asked again.

"Why don't you leave me alone," he shouted pushing her away. "You don't belong to me."

The electric piano in the cafe crashed away without let-up. The place was open all night and everybody likes to hear good jazz music. Upstairs over the cafe there were six or seven rooms with beds and washstands in them. Sometimes when the piano was not playing and the crowd was quiet for a few minutes you could hear a lot of noises up there. An iron bed would fall down making a crash like a locomotive backing into a string of loose freight cars. Or somebody who was good and drunk got mad about something and broke out the windows and smashed the washstands to pieces. The cost of hiring a room was only a dollar. The girl you found waiting asked for five dollars but nobody ever gave one of them more than two or three. Kroot went up and collected a dollar of that.

"I hated to see you get beat up like that," she persisted in saying.

"What do you care about me?" he said pushing her away again. "You don't belong to me."

Somebody upstairs raised a window and emptied a bowl of slop in the alley.

"How does your head feel now?" she asked.

"It hurts like hell," he said rubbing the back of it with his hands.

"Shouldn't you go home and go to bed? You'll feel better in the morning if you do."

"I ain't got a home. Hell."

"Where do you live?"

"Anywhere. Any place I've got the price."

"I've got a place where you can sleep," the girl said. "Will you go with me? You may get hurt if you stay out on the street tonight. You feel dizzy, don't you?"

"I feel like hell."

"I've got a place you can sleep and rest up until you feel better."

"Where is it?"

"Around the corner."

She helped Blondy on his feet and put her arm around his waist. They went out into the street and down past the cafe entrance. At the corner they turned and went half a block to the door of a building that looked like a warehouse from the outside. She unlocked the door and they stumbled in the darkness up the creaking stairway.

There were no lights until they reached the fifth floor where she opened a door and lit an oil lamp.

Blondy fell in a chair and held his head in his hands. The climb up the stairs made his head whirl 'round and noises ring in his ears. The girl stood by the table watching him until he looked up from the floor.

"I'll get you something to drink," she said going off into a dark room. "It will make you feel better. They hit you too hard, damn them."

Blondy sat motionless in the chair and looked around the room. The oil lamp lit it unevenly.

The girl came back into the light with a glass of whiskey. After he had taken it from her she went to the washstand and wet a towel. She came back and held it against his forehead. It felt good.

"What's your name?" he asked looking not at her but at the whiskey in the glass.

"Elsie," she said. ". . . But it used to be Louise."

"What made you change it?"

"I don't know . . . I'll change it back some day."

"Hell. Louise is better than that," he stated.

She hurried around the table and stood between him and the lamp.

"Do you like it?" she asked eagerly.

He leaned back in the chair and rubbed his neck and head. The girl went over to the bed and sat down watching him. The room was cold. He did not answer her.

Neither he nor the girl spoke. Blondy sat with his arms on his

8

knees holding his head in his hands while she watched him. Every few minutes the building was jarred by five or six roaring crashes. Occasionally when there was a lull in the noise below, the electric piano in the cafe around the corner could be heard.

"What do you do?" Louise asked.

Blondy looked up at her. His eyes were blinded by the flickering yellow light and his face was twisted with pain. Across his forehead lay a scar of bruised purple skin.

"Nothing. I used to be a pug."

"A pug?" she repeated. "Then why didn't you beat them up instead of letting them do you like that?"

"I aint a pug no more. The bastard who was running me sold me out."

"What do you mean?"

"The bastard who was running me sold me out. He handed me some dope and rode off on the other fighter. He framed me. He gave me something that made me dizzy and the other pug knocked me out the window. Now I can't get no more fights."

"I'll bet you could if you had a good manager."

"Nobody'll take me on. They think I laid out the last time."

"What are you going to do?"

"Nothing. I'm a bum. I can't get no more fights."

Another crash rocked the building until it seemed as though it would crumble to the ground. The noise it made rumbled away into the night like mountain thunder. Dynamite deep in the ground makes the same kind of sound if you are close enough to hear it.

"You had better go to sleep," Louise said standing up by the bed. "You'll wake up feeling a lot better in the morning."

"All right. Where do I sleep?"

"Here in the bed."

"Where you going to sleep?"

"I'll make a bed on the floor and sleep there."

"Like hell you will! You get in the bed and I'll sleep on the floor. I'm used to it."

"We'll both sleep in bed then," she stated.

9

Blondy glanced around the room seeing the greater part of it for the first time. An empty coal hod sat in the corner by the fireplace. A rusty radiator against the wall by the door looked cold. He went over and touched it. It was colder than his hands.

"All right. I'll do that," Blondy agreed undressing hurriedly.

"I have only two blankets," she said apologetically, "but I'll get my coat. That will help a little."

The jazz-sound from the electric piano was getting louder and more distinct. It came through the thin walls and sounded near as the floor below.

The girl took off her shoes and stockings and got in bed. She slept in her clothes because the two blankets were never warm enough.

Blondy took off all his clothes except his trousers. Then he put his shirt on again. It was getting colder every minute. A shiver ran through the inside of him.

He blew out the light and lay down beside her.

3

Salty Banks sat in a pool room down near the river on Meldon Street waiting for a fighter named Knockout Harris. Salty tossed a pair of ivory dice on the green cloth to pass away the time.

Knockout Harris was a negro middleweight. Salty Banks was managing him.

Salty had something important on his mind and he was waiting for the negro to tell it to him. He had a plan to make a lot of money. The scheme was to let Knockout, who was up pretty close to the top of the division, take a fall. First both of them would cover as many bets as they could get and then collect on the winner. Knockout was not going to be the winner. He was going to lose. And then Knockout would come back and win a second fight and they would collect on that too. The most important part of the plan was getting the right man to work with them. Salty had been doublecrossed too many times to make the mistake of getting mixed up with the wrong man. He had to be right. Knockout was all right. He would stand up. The third man was the one to worry about.

Salty sat on the pool table throwing the dice. Knockout had just won a ten round semifinal two nights before at the big heavyweight championship fight in Cleveland. The bout was merely a preliminary scrap and very few men had noticed Knockout. Later some of the newspapers had brought it up and said Knockout looked like he was through. In a day or two the papers all over the country took up the statement and now the impression was general that Knockout Harris was slowing up. Salty knew it would be easy now to let the negro take a fall and get away with it. And most important of all the bets would be easy to get now. They would cover them all while the money was out and collect on the other man. Knockout had a ten round fight in Philadelphia the following week and when that was over they would play their little game. It was easy. They would clean up fifty thousand dollars on the two fights. Salty was feeling good about it.

Salty tried to think of a fighter in the division with whom they could work but he was afraid of them all. No matter who the third man was they would be taking a chance because he might decide not to come through with the second fight. There was where the trouble lay. Salty hoped Knockout knew a middle who would work with them.

Knockout came walking in the pool room looking for Salty. He had on a new gray suit, a tan derby that lay on the back of his head, and a gold handled walking stick. He bought a new outfit every two or three weeks.

"Where in hell have you been all day?" Salty asked him.

"Ah been to see my woman. That's where Ah been, man."

"I thought you were going to lay off that slut till you got back from Philly next week. What about it?"

"Ah'm all right Salty. Ah could go twenty rounds with the champ right now."

"You won't last five if you don't stay away from her. You can't do that and win your fights too. What about the liquor? I guess you've been on the waggon!"

"Ah took just a little bit in the bottom of a glass last night. That's all Ah've had Salty."

"All right. But if you don't lay off that wench of yours you'll take a fall next Friday night, I'm telling you." Salty wanted to cross-up the men on the inside.

Knockout pulled out a silk handkerchief and dusted his shining tan shoes. He had on a green silk shirt with orange stripes running through it. His face looked sweaty. It always did.

"I've got something to talk to you about, Knockout," Salty told him taking his arm and leading him to the row of chairs against the wall.

"What is it?" Knockout asked.

"Look here Knockout," Salty whispered confidentially, "what do you say we make a killing?"

The negro opened his heavy mouth and closed it. He leaned closer to Salty. His lower lip was so thick it curled under and touched his chin.

Salty continued: "What do you say to cleaning up on the next fight after Friday night?"

He paused a few moments to let the suggestion work its way into Knockout's mind. Knockout leaned closer to Salty.

"I'll fix it with a middle for you to take a fall for a month or two and then come back. See? We'll make a killing both ways. There ought to be twenty-five thousand apiece in it for us. What do you say?"

Knockout uncrossed his legs and inspected the knife blade crease in his trousers. His heavy mouth opened and closed automatically. He wiped his sweaty face with his silk handkerchief.

Slowly Knockout began to speak: "Ah don't know Salty. Ah's a little scared of taking a fall for another guy. They might double-cross you."

"Look here Knockout," Salty said shaking the negro by his coat sleeve. "I'm not going to doublecross you. You know me. It's the other middle. See? It's him we'll give the works. I'll fix him for the second fight. See?"

"How much money did you say Ah'd get?"

"Twenty-five thousand. Look . . ." he said taking a pencil and writing out the figures on an envelope. "See how it looks!"

"That looks mighty good to me."

"All right then," Salty said. "It's a go. We'll clean up fifty grand between us and split two ways."

"All right," the negro agreed. "Ah'll do it if Ah'll get mine without no trouble."

"You'll get yours Knockout. But say. Do you know a middle we could fix it with?"

The negro middleweight sat staring at the floor. He knew all the fighters in the division. He had been in the ring with them all from the champion down.

Salty sat close watching the negro think. Knockout was a good fighter. There was a good chance of him being the middleweight champion some day if he took good care of himself.

"Look here Salty," he said suddenly clutching at the thought in his mind. "Ah knows who we wants to get. He's the middle we want. Don't you remember a fighter named Blondy Niles about two or three years ago?"

"Sure I know Blondy Niles but he aint no fighter now. He quit. He got soaked the last two or three times he started."

"Well him's the middle Ah wants to fight."

"Hell, I don't know where he is, Knockout. It might take me a year to find him. And he might be dead by this time anyway."

"He's the one," Knockout reiterated. "He's the middle to fix it with. He's the fighter we wants."

"All right," Salty said. "I'll see if I can find him but I don't like him none too well. But if I can fix it with him it'll be all right with me Knockout."

14

"Ah gets my twenty-five grand even if something goes wrong with the last fight, don't Ah?"

"Sure you get yours if it goes through. Now listen: You lay off that wench of yours till after the fight in Philly Friday night. You got to come through with a knockout in the sixth round. Because if you don't we can't go through with these other fights. See? We got to get the bookmakers crossed-up. Now you get a knockout before the seventh and I'll guarantee you your twenty-five out of the next two fights if you do just as I say. Let me do the fixing. Let me do all the worrying and take care of everything. I'll take care of your woman for you. Don't you worry about her. You get a knockout before the seventh in Philly and we'll clean up with this Blondy middle inside of two months. It'll be a killing. I'm telling you."

"Ah'll keep rosy, Salty. Ah'll be in condition." The negro hesitated: "But don't you fool with my woman, Salty. Ah can't let you do that."

"All right then. Everything's fixed good and tight. Now I'll go out and turn over some logs and see if I can find this Blondy Niles. When I find him, Knockout, I'll fix it with him just like you would want it. Let me do all the worrying there is. You stay off that wench."

Salty went through the back door to the saloon. There was always a crowd of men there who could tell him anything he wanted to know. They were the wise men. They were on the inside. They were bulb-eyed.

4

Louise lay wide-eyed awake in her bed listening for the sound of Blondy. He had been gone nearly a week already. When he left he did not take his overcoat, saying he would not need it for a while. He did not even say where he was going or what he was going to do. He simply left his overcoat in the room and walked out.

The weather was below freezing. Snow had fallen again the day before and the temperature had gone lower during the night. The men who worked downstairs had gone away and there had been no heat in the radiators for two days. There was no money to buy a hod of coal.

It was cold in the room.

Just before Blondy went away Louise had told him about herself. She realized now how unnatural the story must have sounded to him. When he got up and walked out he looked at her as if he thought she was lying to him. "My God!" he said to himself when she told him she had become a prostitute because she wanted to be one. "My God!

What did you want to do that for?" he asked in a whisper so low she knew he did not want her to answer. She wanted to tell him that she had been lonesome but he got up saying "My God!" again and walked out leaving his overcoat. He had been away ever since. She wished he would come back.

Lying awake in bed waiting for Blondy to come back she brushed a tear from her eyes. She liked Blondy a whole lot. She wanted him to come back. The winternight wind moaned around the corner of the building behind her head. It was becoming colder in the room.

The noises in the building and around it continued. There had been no explosive noises below because the men who worked there were away, but the dull heavy thud of heavy freight being moved in and out of the building resounded on every floor. Trucks backed up to the building and the men got out and worked most of the night with the heavy freight.

Sometime after three o'clock Louise heard the doorknob turn softly in its socket. Presently the door was closed and Blondy tip-toed across the room in the dark. She could not see him but she felt his big shadow over her. When he found the bed by feeling in the darkness he touched Louise in it. His hands were large and cold. She felt his fingers touch her body and an arm pushed gently around her neck. She heard him whisper hoarsely to himself: "Louise! Louise!" This was the first time he had ever touched her. Suddenly his lips searched in the darkness for hers and he was kissing her strongly. His whole body was hard with muscles.

Louise lay motionless not speaking. Blondy put his other arm around her and drew her so tightly to him that he hurt her. For several moments she could not breathe. Only when the heavy chest above her contracted could her own lungs inhale. There they lay each against the other: Blondy on his knees beside the bed and Louise crushed by the strength of him.

"Where have you been Blondy?" she asked breathless.

"Louise," he whispered hoarse, "I had to come back to see you. I had to come back."

17

"What have you been doing Blondy?"

"I don't know. But I had to come back to see you. I had to come back."

His face was cold and his coat was wet with melted snow. He unbuttoned his coat and turned down the collar. His hands were becoming warm under her body.

Louise lay breathless. The pleasure of having Blondy back again made her tremble with delight. She hoped he would not go away in the morning as he did before. She wanted to be with him all the time.

Blondy stood up and took off his wet clothes. She could smell the cold night air in his tousled hair as he bent over untying his shoes. Hastily he lit a cigarette and sucked it half a dozen times without taking it from his lips. Then he threw it out the window where it dropped into the icy river water.

Blondy threw his wet clothes across the room in the darkness. A flurry of snow blew in the open window across the bed. Somewhere below in the night a locomotive whistle sounded three long sharp wintery blasts. Had it been summer there would soon have been the first light of morning in the sky. The loose window panes rattled in the wind.

Louise moved over to the other side of the bed and drew Blondy down between the sheets she had warmed for him. His body was cold and damp and the warmth of her made him shiver involuntarily. She rubbed his cold legs with hers until he was warmer.

Blondy put his arm around her neck and drew her close to him. She lay against him with her legs warm and soft.

"Gee but you are nice and warm Louise," he whispered to her. "I wish I could have been here sooner."

Louise began to cry softly: "You aren't going away again in the morning, are you Blondy?" The tears rolled from her cheeks and fell against his face.

"Do you want me to stay?"

"Blondy you know I can't get along without you now," she said brokenly. Her whole body was shaken with sobs she could not hide. "I missed you so much. Why didn't you come back sooner?"

"I couldn't. But I won't stay away that long again . . . if you want me to stay."

"Blondy please don't leave me again. I missed you so much. I don't want to live without you now. I . . . I . . ." Sobs rose from her body and choked the words in her throat. Tears fell from her eyes and made his face wet with them. He kissed her eyes and tried to tell her he would never leave her again. She clung to him desperately holding his face pressed against hers.

"Louise I love you a lot."

"Blondy I never felt like this before . . . there's something . . . something different . . . I didn't know it could be like this. It's like heaven . . . it's perfect like this . . ."

He kissed the tears from her eyes and cheeks and held her lips against his. She held his head tight in her arms.

"I didn't know kisses were like this," he whispered hoarsely to her. He held her tighter to him.

"And I didn't either. I didn't know they were like this . . . This is like heaven, Blondy!"

The winternight wind was driven against the corner of the building ripping itself apart on the sharp edge of the wall. The sound it made was like the frightened cry of young wolves lost at night in the snow.

She pressed her shoulder closer to him. She felt herself growing to him. Every inch of her body wanted to be touching his.

"Blondy, I love you too," she whispered against his chest. "I never knew it would be like this though. Nothing could be sweeter than this, could it, Blondy?"

They drew closer to each other, desperately, as if they had suddenly been pulled apart. Her body seemed to be growing closer to his each time she breathed. His arms were like steel in their strength. He tucked the blankets around her neck and shoulders tenderly.

"I don't want you ever to go away again, Blondy. I was so lonesome all the time. And it was so cold here by myself." He drew her closer to him.

19

5

Blondy and Louise sat with Salty Banks at a table in the cafe. It was midnight and the place was crowded with men and women who lived most of their lives after sundown.

"Well," asked Salty. "What do you say?"

Louise looked at Blondy urging him.

"There's about ten thousand in it for you if you go through with both fights and put out a few bets right."

"You'll do it, won't you, Blondy?" Louise whispered across the table. "It's a chance for you to come back, Blondy."

"I want something to eat," Blondy answered. "I'll let you know then. I'm hungry."

Salty called a waiter to the table.

"You'll do it, won't you, Blondy?" Louise begged.

"Maybe," he replied reading the menu card.

"I want a sirloin steak," Salty told the waiter, "but bring it out here before you cook it. I want to look at it first."

Blondy and Louise ordered what they wanted. Salty was paying for it. He had a six hundred dollar roll of money in his pocket tonight. The electric piano was playing a new tune tonight. Kroot had bought some new rolls of music and oiled the squeaking parts. A girl got on the floor from one of the tables and tried to dance but she was too drunk. The men carried her back to the table. She had a green silk ribbon tied around her right leg high up on her thigh. The ends of the ribbon hung down below the hem of her skirt.

The waiter brought the thick slice of sirloin on a blue platter. Salty turned it over with his fork and inspected the grain in the meat. The grain ran across the broad slice in narrow parallel lines.

"You've got to select a piece of meat like you do a pair of shoes," Salty explained engrossed in the steak before him. "Now, see this marking? That's a point to remember. When the meat is sliced this strip should bleed for half an hour. This other strip shouldn't bleed at all. Now I'll tell you why. Listen."

He pointed out the two portions of the steak. The meat was marked by several different shades of red. Where it bled it was vivid in color. Elsewhere it was darker and coated with a sheet of black dried blood. The waiter stood pop-eyed.

"Now look," he pointed with his knife bending over the steak. "See that strip there? That's getting hard. Like blood dries in a cut on your hand. When it dries so hard you can scrape it off with a knife it's ready to cook. At least that part of it is. Now look at this other strip: it's still bleeding. See? See how the blood oozes out like a knifecut in the arm? It's still running. When it gets ready to stop bleeding the blood gets thick like molasses and then it's time to throw it on the fire."

The pop-eyed waiter stood beside Salty looking at the slice of raw steak. He looked first at Salty and then at the steak as though he was not sure he was not being made to appear silly.

"All right waiter," Salty said after another moment, "now take this steak on the run and throw it on a quick hot fire for three quarters of a minute on each side. And don't cook it no longer than that. You ruin that steak and I'll have to ask the champ here to take a few swings at your parking lights."

21

The waiter picked up the plate of steak and ran toward the kitchen. He glanced over his shoulder just as he went through the swinging door to see what kind of an expression was on Salty's face. Salty was more or less particular about his food.

"That's the way to have your meat cooked," he told Blondy and Louise. "It's like picking out a pair of shoes. You've got to get the right grain in the meat and then you've got to cook it at the right time. About half an hour after it's been cut from the block is the right time to put in on the fire, but the only sure way is to watch it bleed."

Louise waited for Blondy to tell Salty he would take the two fights with Knockout Harris. She was afraid he would not take them. He was not sure of himself now. He had not been in the ring for nearly two years.

Salty watched Blondy from the corner of his eye.

"How would you like to give your girl a big diamond?" Salty asked intimating that he might give her one himself if Blondy did not make the money to buy it with.

Blondy looked across the table at Louise. Salty had hit upon a tender spot.

"And I'll bet she would like to have some new silk underwear under her dress too," he added. "Who's going to buy it for her?"

Blondy lit a cigarette with jerky fingers.

"If you don't give it to her somebody else will," he concluded insinuatingly. "How would you like to see some other guy taking off her clothes and putting some new silk underwear on her, Blondy?"

Louise looked from Salty to Blondy uneasily. She did not want anybody talking about her like that. She belonged to Blondy now.

Blondy could stand it no longer. He crushed out his cigarette on the bread plate.

"All right," he said nervously. "All right! I'll do it. Get out the papers."

Louise patted his arm and smiled at him.

"I knew you'd do it, Blondy," she said. "I knew you'd want to come back."

Salty spread out the agreement on the table and offered Blondy a pen. There was nothing in the contract about letting down on the last fight. Salty already had another scheme for that one.

Blondy scrawled his name on the paper. Knockout Harris' was already there. The signatures were witnessed.

"When is this fight coming off?" Blondy asked. "I've got to have time to get in condition. I haven't had a pair of gloves on in nearly two years."

"How long do you want?" Salty asked.

"He's got to have plenty of time to get in condition," Louise said. "About three months."

"Three months!" Salty repeated. "Good God! The first fight has got to come off inside of a month anyway. Two weeks would be just right for me and Knockout."

"You've got to give him a chance to get in condition," Louise stated emphatically. "Blondy can't fight like he is now. He wouldn't last out the first round."

"Make it six weeks then."

"Can't do it," Blondy said decisively.

"Two months."

"I might get around in two months and then again I might not," Blondy said.

"I can't let my fighter stay idle any longer than that," Salty said. "If you can't get ready in two months I'll have to find another pug."

"He'll do it," Louise promised. "He'll be ready to fight Knockout in two months."

The man who ran the cafe came in and looked at Blondy. Kroot was ready to throw him out again if he made any trouble. Kroot had a thirty-six strapped around his chest and a pair of brass knucks in his coat pocket.

6

Salty with his bloody steak was the last to stop eating. He talked to Louise while Blondy was thinking about the fights.

"Look here Blondy," Salty said suddenly as if he had luckily remembered something of great importance. "Let's have a celebration tonight. I'll call up Knockout and we'll go out to a place where we can get some good beer. What do you say?"

Blondy looked at Louise. He wanted to go home with her tonight. He had been planning that subconsciously all evening.

"Go on Blondy," Louise urged. "It will do you good. You'll have to begin training soon and you'll wish you had gone." Turning to Salty: "You are paying all the bills, aren't you?"

"Sure I'm paying all the bills. All of them. The treat's on me tonight."

"All right," Blondy said. "I'll go."

Louise got up from the table. "I'll see you later, Blondy. I'm going home now."

Blondy walked to the street with her. He had his arm around her waist. He wished he had not agreed to go with Salty. He wanted to go with Louise. He had been thinking about that in the back of his mind all evening.

"I'll be back soon. I'm not going to stay long, Louise. I'd rather be with you."

She kissed him and went down the street.

When Blondy got back to the table Salty was at the telephone talking to somebody. He came back to the table after five minutes.

"Knockout will be here in a few minutes," Salty said.

"Where are we going?" Blondy asked.

"Out to a roadhouse. It's run by a friend of mine. He'll give us the house if we want it. It's a good joint. Anything you want. Ask for Peggy Joyce and they'd send a taxi after her. They'd get Eve for you if they could reach her on the phone."

They waited ten minutes before Knockout came. He kept the taxi waiting and they went out and got in. It was after one o'clock before they reached the roadhouse.

Salty went in ahead while Knockout and Blondy followed. He went through a door behind the bar into his friend's office. A jazzy orchestra was playing upstairs.

Salty and his friend the owner came out in a few minutes and everybody had a couple of drinks at the bar. The owner was fat and rosy. His paunch was so large the only time he ever saw himself below the waist was when he looked in a mirror. His name was something Jocas.

"Some high class whoopee joint you got here," Knockout told him. "What makes the whoopee?"

"That's what we came here to see about," Salty said.

Jocas took them down a long hall past several doors. There were several parties going on.

Jocas opened a door near the end of the hall and went in. The room had just been vacated and two maids were cleaning it up. A large round table covered with green felt was in the center of the room. Chairs surrounded it. A leather covered lounge and a cupboard were the other pieces of furniture. A closet and a bathroom opened on the right. The maids adjusted the chairs around the room and went out.

"All right, make yourselves at home," Jocas told them pushing a bell button in the wall. "Now what will it be?" he asked Salty.

"Everything," Salty said. "Everything for three and make them man-sized."

A waiter brought in half a dozen brands of liquor and placed the glasses and bottles on the cupboard. He uncorked two of the bottles and passed the glasses around on a tray.

"Hot damn!" Knockout shouted. "This is where Ah been wanting to be for the past two months. You aint going to get me out of here till Ah's dead or passed out."

"You go light on them drinks," Salty scowled. "You're a fighter."

"Ah can win my fights. You keep this merry-go-round spinning and Ah'll win my fights."

"Bring me a blond," Salty told Jocas. "About twenty and plenty hot. I aint felt skin without whiskers on it for a month or more."

"What will you gents have?" Salty's friend asked.

"More of the same and plenty of it," Knockout shouted at the ceiling. "She's got to be hot just like she was sitting on a stove."

"What do you want?" he asked Blondy.

"Anything."

"More of the same and plenty of it," Knockout shouted again, swinging his fists at the overstuffed chairs.

Jocas went out; in a few minutes the three girls came in the room. Salty pointed to the one he thought he wanted and told her to come over to him. He put his hands under her dress and felt her hips and breasts.

"Just right," he said sitting her on his lap. "Curley-head," he pointed to one of the other two, "go over and spill yourself on Blondy."

The girl sat down on Blondy's lap and put her arms around his neck. Her breath smelled of whiskey.

"How are you, Big Boy?" she asked him. "How about getting me a stiff drink?"

26

Blondy poured out two glasses of whiskey and gave her one. He swallowed the other.

Knockout was standing in the center of the room with his arms locked around the other girl. She would not let him kiss her but he could do anything else he wanted.

"How about a little dance?" Salty asked the girls.

"Sure," the girl on Blondy's lap said. "Pour out some drinks."

"Oh Christ! I'm tired," the girl with Knockout said. "I've been doing that all night for another party."

"She's always griping about something," Salty's girl said. "Let her alone. We'll do it without her."

"I'll fix her so she'll want to," Salty said going to the cupboard and filling up half a dozen glasses.

The girl took them all as fast as she could empty them. She went with the other two girls to undress in the bathroom.

When they came out all of them took two more glasses apiece. Each of the girls had a brightly colored ribbon tied around her right leg about fifteen inches above her knee. It was a fad. All the girls were doing it now.

Blondy sat watching what was going on. His girl had an orange ribbon around her leg. She poured him a drink and gave it to him. He swallowed it. He was thinking of Louise.

Knockout had his arms around the other girl smelling her scent.

"Let's have the dance," Salty urged.

While he and Knockout clapped their hands together the girls placed their arms around each other's waists and kicked their legs toward the ceiling. They did not mind showing themselves.

Salty gave each of the girls another drink. They pranced around the room stumbling drunkenly against the chairs. The negro tried to catch one but missed her and fell on his face on the floor. He was so drunk he could not recognize his girl. He tilted back his head and tried to distinguish her by her scent.

"Hot damn!" Knockout shouted almost consumed by the liquor. He succeeded in reaching one of the girls and pulled her down on the floor beside him. The other two kept on dancing.

The whiskey was working its way into Blondy. He drained two of the bottles and sat down heavily on the couch. One of the two girls danced in front of him so close he could see the pores in her skin. Bending over him she tickled his cheeks with her breasts. Blondy dug his fingers into her flesh and threw her down beside him. She lay outstretched on the couch beneath him with her arms and legs jerking a rhythm. Somebody switched off the lights in the room.

At daylight Salty came over and shook Blondy by the hair. He motioned him to get up. The dawn of day was beginning to light the room. Blondy got up looking down at the girl he had been lying on. She was asleep and her mouth lay loosely open. The ribbon around her leg had become untied and lay on the floor. Salty pulled Blondy across the room to where Knockout lay with the girl. Both were sleeping soundly.

Salty ran up the window shades and went back to look at the girl beside the negro. Something was wrong with her. He kicked Knockout away and bent over to see her in the dim light. There was a wound in one of her breasts where she had been bit by the negro. The blood had stopped flowing but her whole body was covered with it. Salty kicked Knockout over on his back. His mouth and chest were smeared with her blood.

"Look at what that son-of-a-bitch did!" Salty said clutching Blondy by the arm and pointing at the girl. "Let's get out of here before something happens."

The girl slept with heavy breath. She was the one who had said she was tired.

They dragged Knockout to the bathroom and threw cold water on his face. When he was partly awake they helped him wash the blood from his face and clothes. Both helping, he dressed.

When Knockout was ready they stole out through the window and ran down the road a mile or more where they found a gasoline station. Blondy phoned for a taxi and they waited in the middle of the road until it came. They got in and in fifteen minutes they were back in town.

Blondy got out at the cafe and Salty and Knockout rode off. Blondy went in and drank three or four cups of coffee and shook himself out of his stupor. When he felt better he got up and went down the street toward the building where he had been living with Louise.

The odor of the roadhouse girl clogged his nostrils so badly he had to open his mouth to breathe. He cursed himself for not going home with Louise when she went.

7

When Louise left the cafe she walked slowly down the street toward home. She did not want to be alone without Blondy and she wanted to take as much time as she could in reaching the building. She did not want him to go off with Salty and Knockout but she thought he would have a good time and it was her way of showing that she loved him.

Louise took out her handkerchief and wiped the vivid red coloring from her lips. When she went out alone she had up until now colored her cheeks and lips as brightly as she could. It was the way to attract attention. But now that Blondy was going to stay with her all the time she was no longer the girl who walked up and down the street looking for men. She belonged to Blondy now. She was straight. She was not a prostitute now. She belonged to Blondy.

The sound made by her heels on the pavement echoed up and down the street against the buildings on each side. The sound changed with every step. Once it was a dull heavy thud, next it was a sharp metallic note. Again it was something else. The pavement was unevenly laid. Here was concrete broken and sunken. There were cobble stones that had been dumped in a pile to fill a hole. Again there were bricks soft and dull under the heels. The sidewalks were old. They were damp and dirty.

Unconsciously she glanced over her shoulder. It had become a habit to glance to see if she were being followed by a man. The glance had been hopeful then, now it was frightened. She was straight now; she was no longer a prostitute. If a man followed her she would run and lock her door so he could not reach her. And before she found Blondy she had prayed for men to follow her. Thank God she was straight now and belonged to Blondy.

As she neared the corner she saw a man who was loitering there. She was almost upon him when she saw him and it was too late to cross the street or go back to the cafe. She hurried around the corner toward her door.

The man's hand took hold of her arm and pulled her back to him against the wall.

"Where are you going, Baby?"

Louise tried to jerk free from his grasp. He pulled her closer to him and put his hands on her.

"What's your hurry, Baby?"

Louise tried to get away from the man without having to speak to him. He was trying to make her talk.

"What's the matter, Baby?"

"Turn me loose," she said angrily pulling away from him with all her strength.

The man held her so brutally she bit her lip in pain.

"Aw what's the matter, Baby? I just want to talk to you a little about something."

Louise had never seen the man before. There were always men on the street she did not know. Blondy was the only one she wanted to know now. She belonged to him.

"How about going with you, Baby?"

"Turn me loose or I'll call somebody to help me. I've got a friend up the street. He'll kill you."

"I'll help you, Baby. What do you want?"

The man hung to her. Louise glanced hopefully up the street and down it. She wished Blondy would come out of the cafe and see her. If he did he would tear down the street and put a finish to this man who wanted to go home with her. The street was deserted except for her and the man.

"How about it, Baby?"

Louise tried to twist her arm free. He held her tighter. He was like all the rest of the men. They all said they wanted the same thing in the same way and made the same kind of proposals. Blondy was the only man who was different. She was glad she belonged to him.

"You're a nice looking kid," he stated appraisingly. "How about my going with you for a little while?"

Her mind suddenly reversing its thoughts she remembered how many nights she had walked up and down this same street trying to find a man who would go home with her. She had been hungry then many days at a time and the food she bought with the money saved her from starving. And now she was trying to get away from a man who would give her a few dollars. Now she belonged to Blondy. He was taking care of her and she belonged to him.

"Aw Baby just a little while," he pleaded. "I've got the money."

Just then the slow heavy footsteps of a policeman coming up the street reached her ears. She felt better. He was coming toward them on the same side of the street. He would be in sight in a few moments.

The man who held her heard the policeman coming up the street walking solidly on the pavement. He turned the corner and disappeared from sight. Louise walked to her door and went in the building.

8

Blondy walked up the five flights of stairs and opened the door. He looked first to the bed to see if Louise was awake. What he saw instead hurled him staggering against the wall. Something was wrong.

Running across the room to the bed he rubbed his eyes to clear their sight. He could not believe what he saw. Louise lay across the bed with her head hanging over the side almost touching the floor. The floor around the bed was covered with splattered blood and the bed was wet with it.

The sight was maddening. He hit his head and gouged his eyes in a frantic effort to bring his mind and sight back to him. He lifted Louise in his arms shouting her name, shaking her, slapping her . . . doing everything he knew to bring her awake. When he finished, exhausted by his actions, he saw her head fall limply over his arm. Her neck had spread over his coat sleeve. It had been cut so deeply he could see the opening in her throat. Her body was cold.

Blondy sat down on the bed. He felt as if he had suddenly been wakened in the midst of a horrible dream to find it was real after all. Blankly he sat on the bed looking at the sight before him.

Louise's body was scratched and bruised from face to feet. Her neck was mangled. Her breasts and thighs were cut and gashed. Along the top of her left leg a knife slash had opened the flesh to the bone. Hair had been pulled from her head and was entangled with the dried blood in her wounds.

Blondy sat insanely erect staring at her. Each time he looked at her anew he discovered another and a more horrible mutilation. Suddenly he jumped to his feet and ran down the stairs and out of the building to the street shouting with all the energy in his body until he was stopped several blocks away by a policeman. Unable to speak coherently he ran back with the man and pointed to the body on the bed.

The policeman took Blondy downstairs on a run and blew his whistle until other policemen arrived. He was turned over to one of them and taken away while the others ran up the stairs to the fifth floor where Louise lay dead.

At the jail he was thrown into a cell and left to shout out his agony until his throat could make no sound. Exhausted and delirious he fell into a stupor of deep sleep.

When Blondy awoke it was another day. The sun was setting red in the west while darkness crouched around it waiting to spring upon it and devour it. He felt the last feeble rays on his head and back as he sat on the bunk trying to recall what had taken place the night before. His throat was raw and sore from the shouting he had done. He could not speak. His clothes were torn and dirty. His coat was not on his back. One of the policemen had taken it from him when they saw the blood on the sleeves.

Dazed and delirious he fell backward in the bunk and was asleep again. When he woke the second time it was still another day and two men were standing over him prodding his side with nightsticks.

Still dazed he was led through the cell room out into the street and in another building. There in a court room several score men awaited him. He was lifted into a chair and his head held up by one of the men who had helped carry him there. Everybody was looking at him and one man was saying something to him. He tried to tell the man to speak louder, but when he opened his mouth he made no sound. His blood-shot eyes saw dozens of men looking directly at him. They were looking at him and trying to make him talk. He could not speak.

Another man pointed at him accusingly and said something to the judge sitting high above them all. Another man came up and shook his head and said something to the judge. The three of them talked and argued, looking at Blondy and pointing their fingers at him. Somebody brought him a glass of water and motioned him to drink it. He swallowed it, keeping his eyes on the men who were talking so earnestly and excitedly about him. Another man came up and felt his pulse and listened to his heartbeat. He went up and spoke to the judge. The man then came back and looked down Blondy's throat for a long time and felt the sore tissues with his rough fingers.

Presently the judge motioned him away and he was lifted from the chair and carried between the same two men back to the cell room. Another man came in and gave him a black liquid and dropped some fiery oil down his throat.

Later he lay down wearily on the bunk and closed his eyes slowly. He was sleeping again.

9

When Blondy was a boy at home he went to school and studied his lessons in grammar and history, arithmetic and spelling. He tried to learn everything his teacher said he should. But no matter how hard he tried and how much he studied he could never make passing marks in any of his subjects except geography. In geography he was at the head of his class. He knew more about geography than even the teacher did. He knew the names of all the large rivers, cities, and countries of the world; he knew where rice was grown, where most of the cotton was raised, and where wheat grew best. He knew more about geography than anyone else in the whole school, including the teacher. But he was always trailing in the other subjects.

Once when the entire school had a geography test and everybody stood in a line around the room like a spelling lesson he was the only one standing when the test was over. The teacher tried and tried to think up a question he could not answer but she could not even make up one. When it was over she gave him the prize for being the best student of geography in the school. The prize was a book called "A Child's History of England" and it was brand new with the price mark of twenty-five cents penciled in the back.

The next year when school opened in the fall he was in a new grade but now there was no geography class for him. He had English and history to learn and algebra in place of arithmetic. He asked the teacher to let him study geography but she said no one in the new grade studied geography, and besides he was too old to be studying geography now.

After the Christmas holidays Blondy was so far behind in his English and algebra he was ashamed to go back to school. His father sent him away into the next county to visit his aunt who lived alone.

When Blondy reached his aunt's house he was already homesick, but she would not let him go back. He had to stay in the front and backyard all the time and never went out into the street to play with the other boys. When summer came he was so tired of staying all day long in the yard that he wrote his father a letter asking to let him come home. For some reason his father never answered the letter. Blondy waited every day for the answer but it never came.

Toward the end of summer he was so lonesome where he was that he got up one night and dressed while his aunt slept and left the house. He walked all the rest of the night and in the morning he was several miles away in a strange county. It was near the sea. He could smell the salt water and the land was flat and marshy. All the remainder of the day he walked along the road never seeing the ocean but always near it. Nobody spoke to him.

By nightfall he had reached the outskirts of a large city and there were houses close together on his side of the road. As it became darker he could see a dull yellow-red glow low in the sky ahead. As he walked further the lights began to appear along the side. The road was paved now and streetcars ran through the center of it. On each side there were cement sidewalks. Following the street for block after block he was soon in the midst of a large city with noises everywhere in the air.

Blondy had had nothing to eat since he left his aunt's house. He passed several restaurants and smelled the food inside and saw men and women sitting at tables laughing and eating all they wanted. He did not know what to do. He had no money.

At one of the corners he stopped and asked some men who were talking there where he could get something to eat. One of them pointed to a restaurant across the street and continued talking with the other men. Blondy touched his arm and told him he had no money to buy food with. All the men stopped talking and looked at him and burst out laughing as loudly as they could. Blondy ran down the street looking back over his shoulder at the men still laughing.

Blondy walked and walked looking for something to eat. His feet had blisters on the heels and on the top of his toes where the shoes had rubbed the skin all day while he walked along the road. When he had walked for another hour not finding anything to eat he decided to go back to his aunt's house.

Turning around he started back at once. He went in the direction he came from and walked dozens of blocks that way. But the further he went and the faster he ran the stranger the streets and buildings became. Still hoping to find the road by which he had entered he walked and ran for another hour it seemed, getting hungrier all the time. Some of the streets were dark and shadowy and he was afraid of them.

At last he stopped, bewildered by the city and lost in it. A sob choked his throat. Unable to stand any longer on his sore feet he fell to the pavement sound asleep. He was fourteen years old.

10

When Blondy opened his eyes one of the guards was shaking his shoulder and Salty and Knockout were standing outside the cell looking at him. The guard pulled off the blanket and motioned Blondy to his feet. It was early morning again outside.

"Hello there, Blondy," Salty called. "How you feeling now?"

Knockout Harris stood by soberly twisting his watch-chain around his fingers. He was wearing another new suit.

"You can go now, Buddy," the guard said. "They don't want you no longer. Go in and see the Captain. He wants to ask you some questions."

"Come on, Blondy," Salty said pulling him through the opening in the cell. "It's all over now. I told them you were with me and Knockout all night. It's all right now. They're through with you now."

Blondy leaned on Salty's shoulder for support. He had eaten no food in nearly three days. His knees were weak under him and he had trouble in walking. His head was clear though. He remembered everything now.

"How you feeling?" Knockout asked taking his other arm.

"Did they find the son of a bitch . . ." he clutched at Salty.

"Naw," Salty answered slowly. "They didn't find him. But don't worry about that. What about the fight? How you feeling?"

"I don't want to fight," Blondy stated.

"Like hell you don't!" Salty said shaking him by the arm. "You've got to go through with it now. Everything's all fixed. Forget this dame. She aint no more. She's out. Forget her, won't you? Get down to work for the fight. You aint got much time now."

Blondy was questioned in the outer room by three men. They made him tell everything he knew about Louise. When he finished answering questions they told him to come back when they wanted him again. Salty had put up five hundred dollars bail for his liberty.

They left the building and rode uptown in a taxi to the cafe.

When they were seated around the table Salty moved his chair close to Blondy.

"When you going to get started training?"

"I don't know. Where'll I work out?"

"You can use Knockout's place. He's going to take it easy for a while now. He's in good condition like he is. All the work he's going to do for a while is about half an hour a day. You can use his place."

"All right," Blondy agreed. "I'll start in a few days. I don't feel like it now."

"Aw for God's sake forget this dame, won't you? She's gone, aint she? She aint no more. Why in hell do you want to walk around dragging your butt on the ground because of her? Forget her, Blondy. You've got a couple of big fights coming off soon. You got to get right. She aint no more. Forget the dame."

"Who do you reckon done that to her?" Blondy asked absent-mindedly.

"How in hell do I know? You get to work and get ready for the fights. Forget the dame. She'd have laid you on the shelf with a sore thumb if you had fooled with her much. I know them kind."

"God damn you, Salty! She was my woman, wasn't she? Shut up! If she was yours you'd be raising hell."

"Listen. There aint no dame I'd lose my sleep over. No matter what happened to her. There's plenty more and God damn good ones too. You don't want to keep no woman too long anyway. They get rotten. Change them once in a while and you'll last longer. You keep one woman all the time and you'll look like a faded shirt. I'm telling you. I know."

"Go to hell. I was going to marry her and have some kids."

"Marry her?" Salty laughed. "What in hell do you want to marry a dame for? Christ. You can have all the dames on the block without that. Marry hell! Take what you want and leave them. Give them kids if you want to. I guess I've got a couple dozen scattered around the country now. Most of the dames want them too. That's all right with me. That's the way to have kids. I know."

Blondy ate his food.

"Ah've got a flock of kids scattered around too," Knockout said. "If all of them got together at one time Ah'd have enough to start a movie theater. Ah'm a big-time pappa, Ah is. Ah's so good Ah gets twins about half the time. That's how good Ah is."

"You'd be sitting up in hell spitting out balls of fire about this time next week if me and Knockout hadn't come around and got you out," Salty said. "You know that, don't you?"

"What?" Blondy suddenly sat up realizing the significance of what Salty was saying.

"You was going to get the grips for knocking off the dame," Salty explained carefully. "They had you all set for the hot-seat until I told them you was with me and Knockout at the roadhouse all night. They went out there and saw I wasn't lying about it and then they let you off. Hell, you'd be sitting in hell blowing the smoke off your toes in another week if I hadn't pulled you out of there."

Knockout nodded knowingly.

Blondy ate his meal like a starved man. He knew Salty was telling the truth about him. Salty did get him out of jail. And he knew Salty could have let him go to the chair if he wanted to. Salty did not care what happened to a man.

But Blondy was his fighter now. Salty was taking care of him. He was even bighearted about it.

11

Blondy in his red silk shorts climbed through the ropes and waited for Knockout to get in the ring. The crowd booed him. He was a quitter the last time he had been in there. He laid down. The crowd had not forgotten. Nobody liked him now or wanted him to win. But Blondy was determined to show them. He was coming back. He was coming back and Knockout would be lying on the floor at his feet when he was the winner. He was going to finish Knockout Harris. The crowd was always yelling for a knockout, wasn't it? Well, it would get one tonight. He would make Knockout wish he had never stopped picking cotton down in Georgia. He would send him back down there.

The crowd wanted blood. It wanted to see blood spurt out of Blondy's nose. It wanted to see blood on the ropes. It wanted to see blood spatter down on the ringside seats every time Knockout landed a blow on Blondy's face. The crowd booed and jeered the man waiting in the ring for Knockout Harris.

Knockout climbed in the ring and held up his hands to the crowd. The crowd went wild over him. The crowd had named him Knockout and tonight he was expected to live up to his name. Knockout was feeling good too. He felt like taking on the champion right then and there. But then he and Salty had fixed it between themselves for him to take a fall and let Blondy come back with a win. Blondy knew nothing about that and neither did the crowd. And Blondy was determined to win tonight. He was going to put Knockout out of the game for a month. He was going to hit him hard. The crowd cheered Knockout and booed Blondy. The gloves were laced on.

Knockout sat on his stool across the ring looking at Blondy and smiling. Blondy glared back at him. He was going to finish the negro if his wind held out long enough. He could take all the punches without any trouble. He had the swing in his arms to finish him with and if his wind stayed with him he would do it. He wished Louise could have been there. She knew he was going to win. She had told him he would when they talked about it in the cafe before Salty came that night.

The referee called them to the center of the ring while the crowd went wild over Knockout.

Blondy went back to his corner and stretched his muscles on the rope. His seconds were trying to tell him what to do. He knew what to do. He was going to smear the negro's blood all over the ring.

The bell sounded and a hush fell over the crowd. It was waiting to see who would land the first punch. The crowd wanted Knockout to land it. Blondy was yellow. He quit the last time he started, didn't he?

Blondy ran in and met Knockout with two hard lefts on the body. Knockout danced back smiling over the ropes. He wanted the crowd to think he was playing with Blondy.

Blondy side-stepped around the ring running in and out of Knockout's defense, limbering up his legs. Knockout played with him, watching Blondy's face and feet and working around the ring. Blondy started off too quick for Knockout. Knockout was not used to the pace. But then he was going to take a fall in the third round anyway and it did not matter. Blondy landed two more. Knockout clinched to save himself. When they came together again Blondy rushed him with a mass of short rights and lefts into the body, pushing the negro against the ropes. Knockout clinched again.

Knockout backed away and came in with a jab to the jaw, jarring Blondy to the soles of his feet. The negro could hit. The crowd cheered him and begged him to level Blondy on the floor. Knockout backed away. The round ended.

Blondy rushed in with the bell almost knocking the negro down with the force of his plunge. Knockout backed into the ropes and see-sawed with his right and left. Blondy drew him to the center of the ring and stung him with a dozen blows before he could break away. Knockout clinched again. Coming out of the clinch Knockout landed a right to the kidney that spun Blondy around. It was a hard blow. It hurt Blondy.

Knockout danced away and waited for Blondy to lead. Blondy led. He rushed the negro against the ropes pounding his body with hard rights and lefts until he ducked and doubled up. Knockout came out with his left eye bleeding. Blondy sparred with him for position. Knockout was backing now. He did not like the punches Blondy had in his gloves. They hurt.

Blondy crowded the negro, pushing him into a corner. Knockout tried to slam his way out but Blondy held him with body blows until he clinched. Out in the center of the ring they exchanged blows. Blondy was worrying the negro. He kept on jabbing his chin with a left every time Knockout advanced. It made Knockout mad.

Blondy walked in with a right to the other's jaw and followed it up with a dozen from both gloves that landed on the negro's body and head. Knockout backed away. Blondy followed him to the ropes and landed an uppercut through the defense. Another followed. Another, another. Another. The negro's head was bobbing back and forward

45

like a punching bag. Blondy had him going. A swift right from the shoulder to the jaw finished him. Before Blondy could begin another swing Knockout collapsed at his feet.

The referee counted him out. It was the long count for Knockout. There was no bell to save him.

The crowd stood up and yelled its head off. Blondy the quitter had come back with a knockout that was the hardest in his career. They were with him to a man now.

PART TWO
MRS. BOXX

1

Blondy stood on the corner of Hastings Street and Lincoln Boulevard looking for something to do. He had seen Salty earlier in the evening and had tried to get some money from him. As usual Salty put him off. He said the money was tied up and they would not be able to collect for the fight until next week. Blondy knew Salty was lying to him. Knockout Harris had plenty of money.

Blondy leaned against the lamp post and watched some people crossing the Boulevard. It was too late to go to a show and too early to go to bed. He did not feel like going to the cafe. It was not quite ten o'clock.

Two girls walked slowly up the street waiting for somebody to stop them. An automobile with two men in it stopped and the men talked to the girls for a few minutes and then drove off again. Something was wrong. Either the girls did not like the men and would not go with them, or else the men did not like the girls. That was more like it.

There were so many girls wanting to be picked up a man could take only what he wanted and let the others go. That was what usually happened.

Blondy watched the two girls walk to the next corner and cross to the other side. Then they disappeared in the darkness.

Blondy lit a cigarette and leaned against the iron post waiting for something to happen. His next fight with Knockout was two weeks off. He would have no trouble in beating the negro the second time.

A girl came up out of the night and stopped beside Blondy. She stood at his side waiting for him to speak to her. The light shone brightly down from the globe overhead. Blondy could not see all her features plainly, but she looked all right. He would not be ashamed being seen with her.

"Hello, Blondy," she said after waiting for him to speak first.

Blondy stood up erectly and looked down in her face. She was looking up now and the light fell full on her face. He had never seen the girl before.

"How do you know who I am?" he asked curiously.

"You are Blondy Niles the fighter, aren't you?"

"Sure. But how did you know it?"

"I saw your picture in the paper last week."

"Well, what do you want?"

"Nothing. I thought you might like me."

"That all depends," he stated walking around her. "What are you peddling?"

"Nothing. I'm on the level."

"What do you want to do?" he asked.

"Anything. What do you want to do?"

"I'm going to bed pretty soon," he told her. "Want to go with me?"

"Where?"

"Anywhere. I sleep in a new place every night."

"Come home with me. You can sleep there."

"Fine," he stated. "Where do you live?"

She told him the street. They went across the street to wait for a bus. One came along every few minutes. Blondy stood looking at her.

"My name's Gertie," she told him when they were in the bus.

"Is it?" he asked.

The house was frame and three stories high. It had once been painted white. It was dirty looking now.

"This is where I live."

They went up the steps and into the house. It had a queer sort of odor about it. It was a sharp biting odor like some kind of antiseptic.

Blondy went in the hall behind Gertie and threw his hat on the table. He had been in houses like this before. He wondered how much the girl would ask.

She led him upstairs to the second floor. Lights were burning in the halls.

"This is my room," she said opening the door and switching on the light.

"This looks like a high class hotel," Blondy commented when confronted by the richly furnished room.

Gertie left him and was gone several minutes. Blondy walked around the room feeling the bed and chairs. The chairs were large and deeply upholstered. The bed had two mattresses on it. The room was as nice as one in a hotel.

The girl opened the door and came in with an older woman behind her.

"This is my mother, Blondy," she said by way of introduction. "Mother, Blondy Niles is the fighter who won the other night from Knockout Harris. Remember me telling you about it?"

"You look all right," the woman stated while she examined him with her eyes. "I hope you like it here. Be sure and make yourself at home."

Blondy was disturbed by the presence in the room of the girl's mother. He had heard of men getting shot in places like this . . . or was she merely the woman who ran the house? He went over to the

51

window and looked out. Silently he stroked his hair. The girl's mother went out.

"Say," he asked when the door was closed. "What kind of a joint is this anyway? Was that your mother sure enough? You're not kidding me, are you?"

"Certainly that was my mother," Gertie laughed. "Mother doesn't care. She likes you a lot. She thinks you are handsome. She's glad I brought you home."

"But I can't spend the night here, can I?"

"Certainly. Mother wants you to. She likes you. She'd like to have you spend the night with her," Gertie paused a moment smiling. "Do you want to sleep with her? She's pretty fat. But you may like fat women for all I know. Do you?"

"Where's your old man?"

"Poppa's downstairs. He never comes up here."

"What will he say?"

"Nothing. He doesn't care."

Blondy sat down in one of the large chairs and was silent several minutes. There was someone moving around upstairs. A chair was scraped on the floor and a door closed shut. There was a sound up there like somebody crying.

"What do I do, pay room rent and board here?"

"Of course not. You're staying with me."

Blondy could not get the situation clear in his mind, but he decided to take things as they came. Gertie interested him now even if she did act queer.

"We can't sleep together, can we?"

"We can if you want to."

"What will your old man say?"

"Nothing. Poppa and Mother don't care. Mother would like to have you sleep with her."

"That's nice. I guess I'll stay here awhile then."

It was quiet out here in this strange residential part of the city. There were no noises out here to deaden the ear. It was quiet and still

52

like the country. And yet only a few blocks away an elevated line rose up in the air and in the other direction was a subway.

Blondy sat in the chair waiting for Gertie to come back so he could get in bed with her. She acted like she was light-headed, but that did not matter. She had gone downstairs. The house was quiet and still. But upstairs he could hear the faint sound of somebody walking on the floor barefooted and again he heard someone crying softly. When Gertie came back he forgot all about the noise upstairs and thought nothing more about it.

2

Blondy got up and dressed the next morning in a hurry. Gertie was already up and dressed. She had gone downstairs. Blondy went to the bathroom and washed his face and hands. Then he went down to the first floor looking for the dining room. There was something strange about the house and the people in it. Something was going on that was out of the ordinary. While trying to find out what the strangeness was he discovered Gertie and her mother eating breakfast.

Gertie's mother, Mrs. Boxx, sat at the table wrapped in a green kimono with a pink lace boudoir cap over her head. She was large and stout this morning. Last night she had her corset on. Her hands were small and fat and on her fingers she wore six or seven rings set with stones. One of them was a large diamond. Her feet were in brown felt bedroom slippers.

Blondy passed at the threshold looking at the two women, mother and daughter. Gertie's mother sat facing him at the end of the table eating a soft boiled egg from a coffee cup. She dipped the egg with a spoon and put it between her lips where her tongue rolled it down her throat. Then she swallowed. Her other hand was curled around a plate of toast. The faded green kimono she wore fitted her loosely. It fell open at her throat and the edges were crossed at her waist. Each time she bent over her soft boiled egg her heavy sagging breasts swung away from her chest and hit against the edge of the table rattling the loose lid of the coffee pot.

Gertie was dressed in a lavender silk kimono. Her hair had been combed and brushed and tied with a blue ribbon at the back of her neck. Her hair hung down her back over the chair top. She looked better than a lot of girls but there was still that queer look in her eyes.

"Good-morning, Blondy," Gertie said looking up when he closed the door behind him.

"Come and sit here beside me," Mrs. Boxx said invitingly. "Your breakfast will be ready in a minute." She jangled a small bell at her elbow.

"Don't sit way up there. Come down here by me," Gertie said.

Blondy hesitated between the two. The cook brought in his breakfast on a tray and spread it on the table between the two women. Blondy drew up the chair and sat down.

"How do you like it here?" Mrs. Boxx asked sweetly.

"Fine," Blondy answered. "But what . . ."

"I know what you mean," Mrs. Boxx interrupted. "You want to know what kind of a house this is, don't you? Well, it's a respectable house for one thing. I used to run a different kind of a house before my two girls grew up, but I sold it at a fine profit when they came along. Now I run a house for sick women."

"For who?"

"Sick women," Gertie said.

"Yes," Mrs. Boxx continued, "I have patients here now. They come here for operations."

"Abortions," Gertie whispered.

"It's a respectable house," Mrs. Boxx insisted. "Nothing shady

55

goes on here. We take women in when they want an operation and attend to them until they are ready to leave. They stay on the third floor though and we aren't bothered by them down here."

"What does your husband do?" Blondy asked unable to place the connection of a man who allowed his wife and daughter to take men to their beds.

"Poppa doesn't do anything now," Gertie inserted. "He just sits around and looks after things."

"My husband is disabled. He lives a life of leisure now and we take care of him. He had something happen to him several years ago. It did him a lot of good. He's a fine man now. Just as nice and gentle as a child."

"What happened to him?"

"It was like an accident. Only it was done on purpose," Gertie said.

"I'll tell you," Mrs. Boxx leaned toward Blondy. "It was what they did to him as a man."

"What?"

"You mustn't say anything to Poppa about it," Gertie warned. "He doesn't like to talk about it."

"It was like this," Mrs. Boxx began, tightening her kimono around her breasts. "My husband went down to the South one winter to work in Florida. He didn't have any money so he asked for rides most of the way. When he got as far as South Carolina he stopped one night in a little town and slept in somebody's barn. Now I want to tell you Blondy, my husband has been good to me all his life. Before he went down to the South he used to chase the girls a lot but I knew he didn't mean any harm and I let him do it."

"Tell him what happened in South Carolina, Mother," Gertie interrupted. "You got off the subject."

"Oh, yes. Well. He spent the night in somebody's barn. He slept in the upper part. I don't know what the name for it is. But anyway when he woke up the next morning a girl was up there gathering eggs that the hens had laid. Well, if you knew my husband you would know what he did then. He likes the girls. Too much so, I used to tell him.''

"He did something to the girl," Gertie stated, impatient with her mother's asides.

"Yes, Blondy. My husband raped the poor girl right there. That's what he did. I don't know what made him do it unless he just got beyond control of himself, because as I told you he's always been a good husband. But he raped the poor girl, yes, he did. And then he left the barn.''

"And some men caught him," Gertie added.

"Will you shut your mouth, Gertrude, and let me tell about this? Now you keep still.''

"What happened then?" Blondy asked.

"Well, the girl's mother saw him leaving the barn and she knew her daughter was up there gathering eggs, so she just put two and two together and ran up there as fast as she could. She found the poor girl up there all violated on the floor. She ran out yelling to everybody in town to stop my husband. The men caught him and brought him back to the barn and the girl accused him of the deed . . . but I'll tell you, Blondy, I'll bet she was tickled to death just the same.''

"Mother, tell about Poppa.''

"Shut your mouth, Gertrude! Well, the men put him in an automobile and took him out in the country and operated on him as a man, they did.''

"They used a knife on him," Gertie explained. "They cut him.''

"Yes, that's what they did," Mrs. Boxx said. "They cut him to pieces where it did the most harm and he couldn't be a man any more.''

"And he's still like that," said Gertie.

"And now, Blondy, that's why me and my two daughters do what we want to do. He doesn't seem to care what we do since that happened to him down in the South. I have my men friends come here to visit me and so do my daughters . . . by the way, you haven't seen my youngest girl yet, have you?''

57

"No," said Blondy looking around the room.

"She isn't here now. She's away. She'll be home again sometime soon. You'll have to sleep with her. She's just the cutest thing you ever did see."

"Now, Mother, don't talk like that. You know I brought Blondy here. It isn't fair to take him away like that."

"Now you be still, Gertrude," Mrs. Boxx admonished. "Blondy is going to sleep with me tonight and he can sleep with me every night if he wants to. But when my youngest girl comes you mustn't hurt her, Blondy. She's such a child. You'll promise me you won't hurt her, won't you?"

Blondy looked wild-eyed at Gertie. He had never been in a position like this before. He did not know what to say.

"Who was making all that noise upstairs last night?" he asked Mrs. Boxx.

"Oh, my dear God!" she shouted hoarsely. "I clean forgot about that woman in the corner room. I did hear her call me early last night but I went to sleep. I bet she's gone by now. I'll have to go right up and see about it."

She got up from the table knocking over the chair she had been sitting on and jogged across the room and out the door. She was so heavy she rattled the china in the cupboard when she walked.

"Where is she going?" Blondy asked Gertie.

"Upstairs to see if the woman is dead. There's so many up there we don't have time to wait on them all and one or two die every week. There's nine up there now operated on and two waiting for the doctor to come this morning. We're always crowded. Mother makes a lot of money with them."

Blondy finished his breakfast and lit his cigarette and Gertie's.

"Let's go up to my room," she suggested. "I want to talk to you where Mother isn't around to bother us. She likes to butt into everything that goes on."

They went out into the hall and up the staircase. At the foot of the stairs leading to the third floor Mrs. Boxx stood with something over her shoulder. She was trying to balance its weight so she could carry it. When she saw Blondy she stopped and dropped what she was carrying on the floor. The shape of it was like the body of a woman.

"Who's that?" Gertie asked her mother.

Mrs. Boxx straightened up and fanned her face with the edges of her kimono. Her heavy sagging breasts reached down to her stomach. Her breath came difficult.

"It's that girl from Harpersburg," she said jerkily pausing for breath. "She must have died early last night. I'm sure I remember hearing her call me, but I was so sleepy I didn't bother to go up to see what she wanted."

A door downstairs was blown shut by the wind. The sound of it echoed through the house.

"Look," Mrs. Boxx pointed and unwrapped the sheet from the body. "She was pretty far gone, wasn't she? It wouldn't have done any good to bother with her last night anyway."

She held back the sheet and they looked at the body. Blood poisoning had turned the lower torso black. The thighs were swollen and blue. The poisoning had developed over most of the body.

"What are you going to do with that?" Blondy asked. "Where are you going to put it?"

"Won't you help me carry it downstairs to the cellar, Blondy?"

Blondy picked up the body in his arms and started to the cellar with it. The body was stiff and unbending. The woman was young and small. She had been good looking. Blondy wondered where her husband was.

Mrs. Boxx and Gertie followed behind pointing out the direction to the cellar door. At the door Mrs. Boxx turned on the lights and went down first. Gertie came behind.

"Lay it here for the time being," Mrs. Boxx directed, pointing to a roughly finished table.

"What are you going to do with it now?" he asked straightening up.

"I'll have it taken out tonight. We can't move them in the daytime. The police would see us."

"Where are you going to take it tonight?"

"The men will come for it. I call them up whenever I have one for them. I used to put them in the furnace but the men offered to buy them from me so I stopped doing that. I don't know what they do with them but I think they sell them somewhere. I get five dollars apiece for them and they get a whole lot more. As much as twenty-five dollars if it's a good one. I can't afford to send the bodies back to their homes. They would get the police after me and make me close up."

Blondy and Gertie went back through the house to the room in which they had slept that night. They went in and Gertie made up the bed and straightened the room. When she finished she slipped off her kimono and put on another one. Then she sat down on Blondy's lap and rubbed her wet lips over his.

3

Castrated Boxx could place a match box in the palm of his right hand, close his fingers over it, and make it disappear completely from sight. He could even do more than that: he could put a match box in each of his hands and make both disappear simultaneously. Not satisfied with that extraordinary display of magic he placed two boxes in each hand, making four all together, and caused all of them to vanish with the same hocus-pocus. Unfortunately, he was not equally as dexterous with the two additional boxes and a quick observing eye could see a portion of the last two going down into his coat pockets. But even at that there were very few amateur magicians who had the ability to perform this sleight-of-hand trick so smoothly. He practiced a great part of the time and had several books on the subject of magic. He had been in his younger days, long before his disastrous trip into South Carolina, the chief assistant to Houdini. So he said.

Blondy sat on the back porch with Boxx and they talked about life in general. Boxx was a gifted talker. He had once delivered thirty-seven lectures in nineteen days in twenty-three states when he was substituted on five hour notice to fill the unexpected vacancy in a lecture tour caused by a visiting British man of letters being suddenly seized with alcoholic tremors. So he said.

Boxx was a generous liar.

Mrs. Boxx had invited Blondy to stay and help her with the house. At this season of the year there were generally twelve to fifteen patients in the house all the time. It was now the middle of summer.

Mrs. Boxx came out of the house and stood on the back porch exclaiming over the beautiful summer weather. She liked the summer because autumn and fall followed. She never said why she liked autumn and fall, however.

Mrs. Boxx wanted Blondy to stay and help her. Blondy did not want to stay but there was something about the woman that caused him to want to please her. He did not like her. He hated her. But nevertheless she induced him to stay through the influence of her extraordinary personality. She had only to suggest that he go up and do whatever it was she wanted done and he went gladly. This was all the more strange because she had no hold on him beyond her queer psychic powers. She swayed his will, changed his mind, and dominated him to such a degree that he could do nothing without her association in his mind. Even when he performed some trivial chore on his own initiative he believed that he was doing it because Mrs. Boxx wanted it done.

Gertie was away from home. Blondy had not seen her in a week. Mrs. Boxx took care of him.

Blondy often lay awake at night beside the huge bulk of a woman whose weight sagged the entire bed out of all comfort and proportion and tried to make himself get up and steal out of the house. But he could do nothing like that. She dominated him completely.

Blondy lay awake in bed beside the woman whose body weighed more than those of three women of average size. She turned over and patted his arm and made love to him. She repelled him with her fat hands and foul breath and mountainous body but he returned her lovemaking enthusiastically. It was the way she had with him. He did everything she wanted him to do.

The duties of the chambermaid were now transferred to Blondy. Early every morning he went up to the third floor and cleaned up the rooms, made up the empty beds, filled the water pitchers and carried out the slop jars. When that was done he went into the room that had been fitted out as a kitchenette and washed the blood from the flowered oil-cloth that covered the kitchen table. It was here that the operations were performed. When the table was clean he poured kerosene in the fire-box of the stove and burnt up the blood soaked towels and remains of abortive births. In the afternoon he went down to the second floor and made up the beds there and swept the rooms and hall. At night he did whatever there was to be done. Once or twice a week there was a body to carry down to the cellar and tie up in burlap bagging for the men to haul away in a truck.

Boxx never did anything. He sat on the back porch during the day smoking and talking to whomever would stop and listen. He worried the life out of the cook. She threatened to hit him with her skillets if he did not stop bothering her but threats had no effect on Boxx. He was determined to talk and nothing was going to stop him.

The physician who came to the house every night and morning to see his patients had nothing to do with any of the family. Whenever Mrs. Boxx, Boxx, or Blondy spoke to him he said nothing.

Blondy had forgot about his fight with Knockout Harris for nearly two weeks. It was only two days off now and his condition was anything but fit. The strange part of it was he was unable to do anything about it. He told Mrs. Boxx he was scheduled to fight Knockout Harris Friday night and she told him he could get off at six o'clock but that he had to be back by twelve. It sounded silly to Blondy to hear the woman telling him what he could and could not do and he laughed at her, but the next moment he realized that he would do exactly as she told him. When she said he could leave for his fight at six o'clock he knew he would not leave the house a second before or after the hour. He would stand in the hall by the clock and leave only when the clock had struck three of the six times. It would then be exactly six o'clock.

Boxx took Blondy by the arm and guided him down the cellar steps. When they were halfway down he stopped and whispered to Blondy.

"I've got a sweetheart down here for you."

Blondy looked at the man and drew away from him.

Boxx pulled him by the arm down the steps into the cellar.

"I've got a sweetheart down here for you," he repeated, pointing to the corner where the burlap bagging was stacked.

Blondy allowed himself to be pulled along.

When they reached the corner Boxx stood on his toes and whispered in Blondy's ear: "See? How do you like her? Is she the kind you are used to? If she's not, just whisper to me the kind you do want and I'll get her for you."

Blondy looked in the corner and at Boxx. He saw no girl. The only thing he could see was the burlap bagging. It occurred to Blondy that Boxx had hid one of the bodies somewhere in the corner under the burlap and expected him to have intercourse with it. Boxx urged him on further.

"How do you like her? Her name is Howe."

"Howe? Howe what?"

"How do you do . . . Haw haw haw."

Blondy looked at Boxx uneasily. The man was laughing at his joke as if he would burst. Blondy shook his head and said he saw nothing in the corner.

"There. Lying there. See? Get down there and play sweethearts with her."

Blondy drew back toward the stairs leading up to the kitchen. The man could not make him take a dead woman like that, if that was what he was trying to do. The man was crazy.

Boxx pushed Blondy into the corner again until they were both on the burlap bagging.

64

"Don't be bashful," he said prodding Blondy with his knuckles. "Go on and play sweethearts. I won't tell anybody. Tickle her under her arms. She likes that. Roll her over on her back and play with her. She likes to play sweethearts. I've been doing it with her all morning."

Blondy dropped down on his knees. Boxx stooped behind him.

The cook was walking overhead going from the table to the stove preparing supper. Blondy could hear her heavy footsteps pounding on the linoleum covered floor as she went from one thing to another. There was no girl on the burlap bagging.

"Don't be bashful. Play sweethearts with her. I won't tell anybody about it. Take her umbrella and fold it up first though. Take off her overshoes and raincoat. She's been out in the rain."

Blondy looked down between his knees to see what he could see. It had not rained in three weeks, the grass on the lawns was burning up and the leaves were dying in the tree tops. Boxx was crazy.

"She is an old sweetheart of mine but I've got a new one now and you can have her. She was my sweetheart before I got a new one. I'll tell you about her when we get time. She lives out at the cemetery."

Blondy bent down on his hands and knees. Boxx stood behind him prodding him with his finger knuckles.

"Go ahead and show her a good time. You can do it just as good with her standing up as you can on the bagging if you want to. I know all about her. She was my sweetheart before I got my new one."

Boxx leaned over Blondy's shoulder and nudged him knowingly with his elbow. He was pleased with what he saw. His eyes blinked excitedly and his face reflected his pleasure. Blondy pretended to do what Boxx wanted him to do. Boxx giggled and moved from one side of Blondy to the other, stooping over and chuckling to himself at what he saw. He was having a good time.

After several minutes, Boxx took out his watch and tapped Blondy on the shoulder. Blondy stood up beside him.

"Time's up now. We'll have to go this time and come back again soon. Tell her how much you enjoyed it. Tell her you enjoyed it very much and that you hope she did too. That's right. Tip your hat and give her back the umbrella and raincoat. We don't want her to get wet, do we? Hand her the overshoes."

Blondy went through the motions expected of him. Boxx was delighted. Boxx tipped his hat friendly and bowed low.

When they were halfway up the stairs Boxx clutched Blondy's arm tightly in a painful grasp: "Don't tell my wife about her down here. It would make her jealous. You mustn't say anything about her. We want to keep her down here so we can come back again, don't we?"

Blondy promised he would not tell Mrs. Boxx about the girl in the cellar.

4

Blondy stood before the clock in the hall watching the minute hand move toward the numeral 12. The hour hand already pointed to six. When the bell struck the first of the six chimes he put on his hat. He waited for the second. When the third note sounded he opened the door and ran down the steps to the street.

Outside the house he paused a moment and looked up at it. There was something like death about it. The color was ash gray and it looked a hundred years old. On the top story a dim yellowish light shone through one of the dusty windows. There were no other lights in the house.

Blondy ran down the street toward the subway entrance. When he reached it he disappeared like a rabbit jumping in a hole to escape a pack of howling dogs on its trail. Down inside on the track level he felt secure. There were other people there, men and women whose actions and thoughts were not directed by somebody else. He paid his fare and went out to wait for a train. It came in half a minute. He sat on the edge of the seat waiting for the station he wanted.

Boxx and Mrs. Boxx seemed miles away as he ran up the steps of the arena where he was to fight Knockout Harris. He felt as if he had been sleeping for a month and just woke up in time for this fight.

When Blondy entered his dressing-room, Salty Banks was sitting on the edge of a table talking to two other men. When Blondy entered the room all of them jumped up and stood looking at him with their mouths agape. Salty was the first to regain his speech. He sat down again on the table.

"Where in the name of Jesus Christ have you been?" he demanded, surprised and angry.

"What difference does it make? I'm here now." Blondy was afraid to tell him about Mrs. Boxx keeping him in her house all this time. Salty and the other men would make a fool out of him.

"You're the God damnedest pug I've ever tried to run. Here I've been looking for you in every ash can and garbage bucket in the whole damn town ever since I couldn't find you last week. Where in Christ's name have you been?"

"Listen, Salty. I'm all right. I'm ready to fight Knockout tonight. That's all you care about anyway. I'm ready to fight. See?"

Salty smiled between his lips. He came over and felt Blondy's biceps and thumped his chest and belly with his fists.

"Forget it, Blondy," he pleaded. "I was only kidding you. Sure you're all right. Better take a lay-me-down and rest up for a couple of hours. I've fixed everything for you. I knew you would turn up in time for the show. I pulled one on the Commission. I had them weigh-in a bruiser that's just your size and weight and he looked so much like you they didn't know the difference. If you hadn't turned up I was going to use him with Knockout and nobody would have been wise. Everything's all right now. Take it easy and rest up good."

Blondy took off his coat and unnotched his belt. He opened the collar of his shirt and unlaced his shoes. Then he stretched out on the cot by the window. Salty motioned the other men out of the dressing room.

68

Salty came over and pulled up a chair beside the cot. He bent over toward Blondy.

"How you feeling, Blondy?"

"I'm all right."

"Stomach all right?"

"Sure."

"Hands?"

"Yeh."

"Any soft spots?"

"Naw."

"How does your head feel?"

"Right."

"Hands steady? Hold them out and let me see them."

"My hands are all right."

"Shaking a little, aint they, Blondy?"

"What? My hands? Hell no. They're as steady as a snake's eye."

"Look," Salty said, taking a bottle from his coat pocket. "Better take a swallow of this to steady your nerves."

"I don't need it. What is it?"

"A nerve steadier I got from the doc. He said you'd better take a little if your hands was shaky."

"I don't need it."

"Yes you do. Take a swallow and it'll set you right. I know what's good for you. Take it."

Blondy took the greenblown bottle in his hand and looked at the label. It was blank.

"All right," he said turning it up to his lips.

"That's fine, Blondy. You'll be right in the ring now. You'll feel like a million lumps."

"All right," Blondy said.

"I'm going out now and let you rest up some. If you want anything open the door and call me. I'll be around somewhere."

Salty went out and closed the door. Blondy lay back and closed his eyes. The nerve steadier Salty gave him helped a lot. He felt quiet and still.

Salty shut the door and went down to Knockout's dressing room and told him Blondy was there and had taken a mouthful of nerve steadier. That made Knockout feel fine.

Blondy was awakened an hour and a half later by Salty. He had been asleep ever since Salty went out. Salty pulled him up and shook him.

"Wake up, Blondy. It's almost time to get in the ring."

Blondy rubbed his eyes and tried to wake up. He felt heavy-headed and sleepy. Salty took his clothes off and slapped his body with his hands. The rush of blood from one side to the other made him sit up. The nerve steadier had done its work all right. He was not a bit excited and his hands were steady.

He let Salty bind his hands and lace his shoes. The seconds came in and talked to him and they waited for the call.

Blondy climbed through the ropes and sat down on his stool. Knockout came over and rubbed his hands against Blondy's and went back to his corner.

The fight lasted a minute and a half by the timekeeper's watch. From the stop of the gong until he felt himself sliding down Mrs. Boxx's lap to the floor he had moved around the ring under the force of Knockout's blows. He did not know what was going on.

When he woke up he was lying in his dressing room on a bench. Everybody had left and there was not a soul in the building. The arena had been emptied and only the light in the dressing room was burning.

Getting clumsily to his feet he went over to his clothes and fumbled for his watch. It was eleven-thirty. Tearing off his trunks and shoes he jerked on his clothes as speedily as he could. He had time enough to dash to the subway and get home at twelve, and that was all. He had to be back before the clock in the hall finished striking twelve. He had to be there.

Blondy ran down the subway steps and boarded a train. When he got to his station he ran out and up to the street level. The house was three blocks away and he had three minutes to reach it. He ran as fast as he could.

Bursting open the front door he ran to the clock. It was getting ready to strike. The spring that caused the hammer to strike the bell had been sprung and it was winding preliminarily to striking. Before he could take off his hat and lay it on the table the first tap rang out through the hall. He placed his hat on the table and went upstairs to his room.

Mrs. Boxx looked out her door when she heard his steps in the hall and motioned him inside. She went back and got in bed while he undressed. The clock downstairs finished striking the hour of midnight.

5

The next morning when Blondy went downstairs for breakfast, he found a man he did not know, sitting at the table close to Mrs. Boxx. He was talking to her. When Blondy entered, the man stood up to be introduced. Blondy went to his chair and sat down.

"Blondy, this is Jackie Crawford who is going to stay here awhile with us. Blondy used to be a prizefighter, Jackie."

Jackie came around the table and held out his hand for Blondy to shake. Blondy wondered why Mrs. Boxx said he used to be a prizefighter.

"Just call me Jackie. Everybody calls me Jackie and I like it awfully well."

Blondy took his limp hand and shook it. It felt like shaking a drowned cat. Mrs. Boxx brushed the crumbs away from Jackie's place and held his chair back for him. Blondy drank the cup of coffee.

"Jackie is such a nice gentleman," Mrs. Boxx told Blondy. "He is just like my husband. He is so nice and gentle."

Blondy felt his sore face and side. Knockout Harris's blows were man-sized.

"Jackie was just telling me about himself, Blondy. He said all his life he had tried not to be brutal and rough like other men. Some men are awfully rough with women. My husband is just like a baby with me."

"Oh yes," Jackie exclaimed shrilly. "I was going to tell you, dear Mrs. Boxx, that my greatest struggle in life has been trying to subdue my frightfully rough male passions. They seem to want to dominate me entirely at times but I hold them back the best I can. You know, dear Mrs. Boxx, I never let myself drink ice cream sodas anymore because I have discovered that they inflame my sexual passions something awful. I never touch such things anymore at all. I think that is best, don't you, dear Mrs. Boxx?"

"You are such a dear man, Jackie. So gentle and lady-like. I wish all men were like you. My husband is that way. He is so gentle and nice."

Blondy finished eating his breakfast and went out of the room, leaving Mrs. Boxx and Jackie to themselves. He did not want to have anything to do with Jackie. He hated him.

Blondy found Boxx on the back porch. Boxx told him to sit down.

"I've got something to tell you," he confided mysteriously. "Do you want to hear it?"

"What is it?"

"Lean over here and I'll whisper it to you. I don't want anybody to know I told you. And I don't want you to tell them I told you."

Blondy drew closer to Boxx.

"Do you know what they are going to do to you?" he asked in a low whisper behind his hand.

"What who is going to do to me?"

"They. My wife and Jackie."

"No. What?"

"They're going to take a pair of scissors and make you like me. You know. Like I had done to me."

"You're crazy!" Blondy shouted. "Nobody can do that to me! Do you think I'd let anybody do that?"

Boxx sat back in his chair chuckling to himself. He took out a match box and practiced his sleight-of-hand trick half a dozen times. The cook was walking around heavily in the kitchen.

But the more Blondy sat there and thought about the matter the more uncertain and frightened he became. The power the woman held over him was stupendous. She could make him do anything she wanted him to do. If she had decided she was going to make him submit to that kind of operation she could make him want to have it performed. Blondy suddenly realized the extent of her domination over him and he was frightened. But he could do nothing about it.

Mrs. Boxx came on the porch followed by Jackie. They went to the porch railing and leaned against it looking at Boxx and Blondy. There was a triumphant smile on Jackie's face.

"Come up to my room in about five minutes, Blondy," she instructed him casually as though she had told him to close a door. "I want you to come up."

Blondy sat in his chair looking at her. He could not find the power in him to refuse. He was afraid to say no. She and Jackie went in the house.

Freedom was only over the fence a few yards away. An alley was there that led to the street on which the elevated ran. But he could not move. His body would not respond to the direction of his brain. He sat in the chair. Boxx sat on the other side of him playing with the match boxes in his hands and chuckling to himself.

Blondy sat waiting for the five minute period to end. He would go upstairs. Boxx had told him what they were going to do to him. He had had sufficient warning to get away. But here he sat waiting for the time to go up to Mrs. Boxx's room where Jackie was with her now. He tried to get up and run out in the yard and hurdle the fence, but his body sagged deeper in the chair.

He got up and went in the house to the stairway. Jackie's hat was on the hall table. His own hat was there too. The front door was two feet away unlocked. Blondy went up the steps one at a time. There were twenty-six steps. He counted them. The fifth step from the bottom had a squeak in it near the wall. The sixteenth step was narrower than the others. The edge had been splintered off. The third step from the top sounded hollow when he put his foot on it. The twenty-sixth step was the last one. Blondy put his foot on it and quickly took it off again.

Mrs. Boxx opened the door and crooked the third finger of her right hand at him. She said he should come into her room. Blondy mounted the final step and edged through the door beside her. His body touched her. He had to squeeze through the door with her standing in it. He could not help touching her. She was large enough to fill the door standing sideways in it. Blondy entered the room. There was an open window facing him. He still had a chance to get away. He looked away from the window.

Jackie sat on the bed holding his knees in his hands. Blondy went over to the chair Mrs. Boxx showed him with her finger. It was by the stove. There was no fire in the stove. It was too hot. It was August. He sat upright in the chair facing Mrs. Boxx.

Jackie had a hand mirror on the bed beside him. He picked it up and rubbed the tips of his fingers over his face feeling his skin. He adjusted his necktie and turned his head first to the right and then to the left looking at his ears and as much of the back of his head as he could see. There was always a drop or two of saliva in each corner of his mouth.

Mrs. Boxx crossed the room and stood beside her bureau looking at Jackie and smiling at him. Jackie smiled at her and went over beside her. He patted her stomach and chuckled her under the chin. Laughing coyly she tickled his ribs.

Blondy sat watching Jackie play with Mrs. Boxx. She took Jackie by the hand and led him to the bed and sat down. Reclining on her back she pulled him down on top of her. Jackie tickled her under the arms making her giggle. Her whole body shook heavily, bouncing Jackie up and down and making the bed creak under the strain. Jackie was having a splendid time bouncing around on her barrel-like belly. Mrs. Boxx was having the time of her life.

6

Mrs. Boxx pushed herself into a sitting position and sat Jackie beside her. She told Blondy to come to her. Blondy left his chair and sat between them on the bed. She sent Jackie after the large scissors.

"Blondy, lie down and we won't hurt you," she said placing her hand against his chest and pushing him backward on the bed where she had been.

"For God's sake, Mrs. Boxx, don't do that! Please!" Blondy implored, seeing the big shears in her hands. "Please, Mrs. Boxx, don't do that. Please, Mrs. Boxx!"

Mrs. Boxx was sympathetic but firm. She would not be deterred.

"Don't pay any attention at all to him, Mrs. Boxx," Jackie said indignantly. "He is rude to you. This will make him more gentle."

"Now, Blondy, don't be bad. We know what is best for you. Don't we, Jackie?"

"Yes we do, Mrs. Boxx. Now you behave yourself, Blondy."

"Jackie, you get him ready and I'll cut with the shears." She turned upon Blondy: "Now Blondy, you lie still and we won't hurt you at all. It will be over in a second."

Blondy lay helplessly on his back. The woman sat beside him snapping the shears in her hands. Jackie fumbled with his clothes.

Blondy jumped up knocking Jackie to the floor. He ran across the room and stood back to the wall.

"God damn you!" he shouted at Jackie on the floor. "You keep your rotten hands off me and leave me alone."

Mrs. Boxx adjusted herself patiently on the side of the bed and calmly called Blondy's name. She was not excited nor was she angry. She was merely determined.

"Jackie you go in my closet and bring me that trunk rope," she instructed him with her eyes boring into Blondy.

Jackie jumped eagerly to his feet and went to the closet. Blondy stood erectly against the wall.

"Tie his arms behind him," she instructed Jackie.

Jackie tied Blondy's arms behind his back and waited for further instructions.

"Come over here and sit by me," she told Blondy.

Blondy sat down where she wanted him to sit.

"Now tie his legs together with the other end," she said.

Jackie tied Blondy's legs securely.

"Now we won't have any trouble," she said to Jackie patting his cheek.

Jackie placed his damp white hands against Blondy's neck and pushed him down on the bed. His hands were always cold and moist. He unloosened Blondy's clothes.

"Horrors!" Jackie exclaimed shielding his eyes with his arm.

"What's the matter, Jackie?"

"Look! He is so disgustedly male. I hate the sight of men. They are so animal-like."

"But hurry, Jackie. We have got to finish this."

Jackie turned his head so he would not have to see the sight that upset him so violently. Mrs. Boxx waited anxiously with her shears.

"Are you ready?" she asked Jackie, snapping her shears together.

"Yes," said Jackie clutching at his throat.

Mrs. Boxx bent over Blondy with her shears.

"For Christ's sake Mrs. Boxx!" Blondy yelled with all his strength. "For Christ's sake don't do that! Please, Mrs. Boxx, don't do that!"

The door was suddenly flung open and Gertie ran in. She had just come in the house and heard Blondy's yell. She was so surprised at what she saw she could not speak at first.

"Mother! What are you doing to Blondy?"

"You go out and leave us," Mrs. Boxx told her.

"Stop!" Gertie cried. "You can't do that to Blondy."

"Now, Gertrude, you go on out and let us finish."

Gertie ran to the bed and pushed Jackie off. She jerked away her mother's shears and threw them out the window. She unknotted the rope around Blondy's arms and legs. When he was free he sat up and covered himself with his clothes. Gertie threw her arms around his neck protectingly.

"What are you going to do that for?" she asked her mother.

"Gertrude, I wish you would let me do what I think is best. You have no right to interfere."

"You can't do that to Blondy. I won't let you."

"What have you got to do with it?" Mrs. Boxx shouted at her.

"I won't let you do that to him anyway."

"All right then," Mrs. Boxx said, standing up. "I will wait a few days until you have had enough of him. But I'm not going to wait long. I'm giving you plenty of time, Gertrude. Come on, Jackie," she said taking his arm. "Let's go out now. We'll finish it when Gertrude gets enough of him."

Blondy sat looking at Gertie trying to say something for what she had done. He did not know how to thank her. Anxiously he felt himself all over as if he could not believe he was still alive and whole after the experience with Jackie and Mrs. Boxx. Mrs. Boxx's shears, snapping metallically, still rang in his ears.

"Come to my room, Blondy," Gertie said, putting her arm around his waist. "Let's go in there and talk."

Blondy fastened together his clothes and went with her. He had never in life been so glad to see anyone as he was to see Gertie. She had saved him temporarily from Mrs. Boxx.

7

Sometime in the middle of the night, Blondy was awakened by noises overhead on the third floor. When he first woke somebody was dragging a bed across the room overhead. Several heavy boxes were dropped on the floor shaking dust in his eyes, and two people, a man and a woman, talked to each other impatiently. Blondy lay awake listening now. He was wide awake.

Two people left the room above slamming shut the door. In several minutes they came back, making more noise. More heavy boxes were dropped on the floor. Once again they talked to each other loudly. Blondy sat up in bed and tried to hear what was being said. Whoever it was had no consideration for the sick women trying to sleep.

While he was listening to what was taking place up there, the door of his room was opened and the light switched on. Mrs. Boxx stood in the door fully dressed.

"Get up and come upstairs," she said bruskly. "I've got some work for you to do."

Blondy jumped out of bed and hastily pulled on his clothes. When he tied his shoes, he opened the door and ran up to the third floor.

Mrs. Boxx and Jackie were standing in the hall talking to three women in their street clothes, who leaned wearily against the wall. They looked around nervously when they heard Blondy coming. The men who had brought their baggage had gone.

"Come here," Mrs. Boxx told him.

Blondy went to her side. She had one hand on Jackie's shoulder. The other was supported by her hip.

"We are overcrowded tonight. There are three new ones who just got here and I haven't room for them. You will have to bring your bed up here and put it in the kitchenette."

Blondy agreed with her. Jackie always did.

"Wait," she said indecisively. "Let me see . . . yes, that's right. Go down and bring up your bed and set it up in the kitchenette where it won't be in the way."

The three women patients leaned against the wall and looked frightened. They were ill. Mrs. Boxx made them afraid to be ill.

Blondy went down and carried up his bed piece by piece. Jackie did not offer to help. He stayed with Mrs. Boxx echoing her commands and agreeing with her.

Blondy set up the bed and made it up for one of the women. She sat down on it and began taking off her shoes. She would probably never put them on again.

Mrs. Boxx took one of the other women to the last vacant bed and told her to get in it. The third woman was still without a place to lie down. Two of them could have doubled up but the beds were all single cots and were not even wide enough for one person. Mrs. Boxx came back and looked meanly at the woman leaning against the wall.

"Why did you have to come here when I'm full?" she berated the woman, angrily. "You knew I didn't have room for you now."

The woman pleaded that she knew nothing about the house being crowded. The doctor told her to come, she begged. It did not relieve Mrs. Boxx's anger.

Mrs. Boxx took Blondy to the corner and drew his head close to her mouth while she whispered to him.

"There's a woman in the room next to the bath, who is going to die pretty soon. You take her down to the cellar and put her on the bagging. She may as well die down there as up here when I need room as bad as I do now. She's paid up for the week. I'll put this other woman in her bed while you go down to the cellar."

Blondy followed her directions implicitly. Mrs. Boxx knew what she wanted done. He went to the room where the woman slept. When he turned on the light, she woke. None of the patients in the house ever slept soundly. Mrs. Boxx was always running in and out of the rooms looking for a body to take down to the cellar and get five dollars for.

"Please, for the sake of God! Don't take me out!" the woman screamed. "I know what you are going to do with me! You are going to take me down to the cellar to die!"

Blondy paused beside the bed. The woman was hysterical with fright. Her body was in convulsions. She was not the first one to be carried down there to die on the bagging.

"Holy Jesus! Help me!" she screamed at the top of her voice. "Get my husband to take me away . . . he doesn't know where I am . . . tell him to come for me and save me . . . I want to go home to die where Charlie and my babies are! Oh, please, for Jesus's sake don't take me down there to die. Call my husband . . . he'll come for me and take me home where my dear, precious babies are . . . I can't die and leave them! Charlie . . . Charlie . . . Charlie! Come quick and get me. Charlie . . . Charlie! Please God! Charlie! Please, God, don't let them take me down there to die! Charlie . . . Charlie . . . can't you hear me? Charlie! Please, God! Charlie come quick and get me before they kill me. Oh, sweet God, help me! Charlie . . . Charlie . . . Charlie! My dear precious babies! Oh, please, dear God, send me back to my babies before I die! Tell Charlie to come after me quick. . . ."

Mrs. Boxx came running in the room and slapped the woman's face until she cringed with pain.

"Shut your mouth, you damn fool!" she snarled. "Do you want to let everybody in this part of town hear you! Shut your mouth, you fool!"

The woman looked at Mrs. Boxx through the tears on her face. Seeing the face of Mrs. Boxx so close to her that she could feel her breath against her forehead, she screamed louder and louder. Mrs. Boxx pushed the end of the sheet into her mouth and held it there.

"Pick her up, you idiot," she snapped at Blondy. "Don't stand there waiting for her to wake everybody on the street. Pick her up and carry her down to the cellar, quick."

Blondy drew the cover off the woman's body and picked her up in his arms. Her body was limp from her waist to her feet.

Mrs. Boxx tied the sheet around the woman's face and knotted the ends so it would not come loose. She tied the woman's arms to her side with the other end.

Blondy carried the woman down the stairway to the cellar and laid her on the burlap bagging in the corner. He left her there haunted by her eyes. They were bursting with something she wanted to say.

Mrs. Boxx came to the top of the stairs and yelled for Blondy to hurry back. She had something else she wanted him to do.

Blondy covered the woman with the bagging and left her. Her eyes screamed through his back.

Upstairs on the third floor again he made up the bed for the woman and helped her in it. She was only a child in her teens. She was frightened. She should have been somewhere else. She was not married.

When he finished his work and started back to bed, the first gray dawn of the day broke through the windows. He forgot he had taken his bed upstairs for one of the women. Mrs. Boxx called him into her room.

"You can sleep with me and Jackie," she said.

He followed Mrs. Boxx and Jackie into the room. She took off her clothes and lay down on the bed and Jackie got in beside her. Blondy lay down on the other side. Mrs. Boxx turned over on her side, her back to Blondy, and stroked Jackie's hair. Her body raised the bed covering like tent poles and the ends of it were shortened by the extraordinary size of her body. Blondy was uncomfortable.

Mrs. Boxx and Jackie played with each other for the next half hour. He could hear all they said to each other and he could feel the motions of her hands as she moved them around under the cover. Jackie lay meekly submitting to her play. He liked it.

Blondy lay awake another half hour and then got up. He could not sleep now. The sun had risen and it was day. He went downstairs and waited for breakfast.

8

Boxx was in good spirits today. He was playful and jovial. Blondy felt heavy-headed and tired after his night's work upstairs. After he had eaten breakfast he felt better though.

Boxx told Blondy to sit down in the chair beside him. They were on the back porch watching a man bring some groceries into the kitchen from the alley.

"I visited my first wife again yesterday afternoon," he whispered to Blondy. "It was the first time I had seen her in almost a month. She hasn't changed a bit."

"I didn't know you had been married before," Blondy said.

"Sure. This is my second wife I've got here now. I'll be marrying my third one as soon as this one dies. A man has got to have at least three to amount to anything. They wear out three times faster than a man does."

"Where did you see your other wife?"

"In the cemetery. She lives there now with a lot of other people."

"How did you see her if she's dead?"

"Shh! It's a secret. I've got a private way of getting down there where she is. You know, there are a lot of them down there, men and women. They have a good time too. They have dug out a big room down there and connected up all the coffins with halls. They sleep in the coffins and then walk around visiting each other and meeting in a big room to talk and sing. They have dances sometimes too. They have a good time down there, you can bet your boots! You know, the men and women down there carry on just like they do up here. They have dates and get married and all such things. Only a few of them get married though because, hell, what's the use? If a man and a woman down there like each other that way they sleep together just like up here, but they don't go and get married just because of that. Nobody cares if they get married or not anyway. Everybody tends to his own business and keeps his nose out of other people's business. That's the way to do, too."

"What did you do down there?"

"Oh, I had a good time. A damn good time. I went to see my wife and she took me in her coffin and we stayed there an hour or so. Say, you know, I bought my wife a fine coffin. I didn't think so much about it when I got it, but yesterday when I saw it I was real proud of myself for getting her such a nice and fancy one. It's all padded and lined with soft white silk cloth and fixed up nice. She's crazy about it, too.

"And say, you should see the men down there . . . they are the funniest looking people you ever saw. All of them wear coats with no backs to them and a lot of them have pants with only the top part. But then some of the women wear only a fur coat or a dress with the back cut out too. Most of them have to wear new shoes that pinch their feet pretty bad. It would be all right, but lots of them don't have any socks and the shoes blister their feet pretty bad on top of that. There's one woman down there who had on a pair of her daughter's shoes and they were two and a half sizes too small. It's a shame the way people treat us when we die. They give us nothing but the old worn out clothes to wear with us.

"They have a good time down there when a new grave is dug in the ground. They all stand around waiting to see if it will be a man or a woman. A lot of them bet on which it will be. And then when the coffin is in and covered up everybody helps to open up the side so they can get a look inside and see who wins the bets. If it's a man all the women crowd around and ask him questions and flirt with him. If it's a woman the men push the other women away and go in and ask for dates. But there is one disagreeable thing down there. A lot of people get put in their coffins all butchered up. A lot of them are cut open by doctors and some have lost parts of themselves in accidents. One man down there hasn't got anything inside of him at all. Not even the smallest part that was inside him up here before he died.

"Some of the women look funny in their old clothes. Lots of them have been down there a hundred years or more and their dresses are sure out of date. The newest ones are dressed up in the latest styles though.

"But I guess the funniest thing down there is to see those people who have got only the front part of their clothes on. You see a man coming walking down the hall toward you all dressed up in a fine looking suit of clothes and then when he passes you and you look back at him, he's as naked behind as he was the day he was born. The women are the same way too. That is, some of them are. But a lot of them have got dresses with only the front part. They walk around all naked behind and don't seem to care at all if they show that part of themselves. But then it's not their fault. It's the clothes their folks dressed them in when they died. They couldn't do anything about it if they wanted to."

Mrs. Boxx suddenly appeared on the porch, interrupting Boxx in the midst of his recital. She told Blondy to go down in the cellar and see if the woman he took down there last night was dead yet. She waited until he left.

Blondy went down where he had laid the woman on the bagging. She had rolled off the pile and lay on the floor dead. She had doubled herself into a knot. He called Mrs. Boxx and she came down.

"You'll have to straighten her out," she said looking at the body.

"The men won't take her out looking like that. They have to have a straight piece so as to look like a rolled-up rug."

Blondy stooped over the woman and pulled out her feet. The body was stiff and unyielding. Mrs. Boxx called Boxx to come down and help them.

"Turn her over," Mrs. Boxx directed.

Boxx came down the stairs.

"Now," she said when they had all gathered around the body. "You hold her shoulders down to the floor," she told Boxx. "And you pull her legs out, Blondy. I'll sit on her and help bend her down."

All three went to work on the stiff body trying to make it straight so the men could carry it out looking like a rolled-up rug. It was a hard job with the woman's body. The joints cracked when they worked on her and the taut muscles in the legs were tight until they broke under the strain and allowed the knees and hips to straighten out on the floor. Blondy was sweating with his exertion. Mrs. Boxx sat her heavy rump on the woman's back and her weight pushed it down until the stomach touched the floor. Boxx held the shoulders to keep the body from slipping sideways. Blondy had done all the work on it.

At last they succeeded in straightening the body to give it the appearance of a rolled-up rug. It was Blondy's job now to roll the burlap bagging around the body and sew it up with the big blunt needle and hemp twine. When he finished, it was ready to be carried away by the men when they made their call that night.

He lifted the body on the table where the men could get it easily. Then he went upstairs.

9

"Hello," said a girl's voice from the door.

Blondy sat on his bed looking out the window. Over the roof-top next door he could see the ending of the city's suburbs in the distance. Away off in the open country the fields lay green and the hills round and wooded until they all faded into the sky.

He turned around at the sound of the voice. It was strange to him.

"I'm Dorothy." She paused. "Gertie's sister."

Blondy went over beside her. She had something about her that attracted him. Her voice was soft and musical and her smile warmed him. He thought she was beautiful.

"I'm Gertie's sister. She told me about you. It's a shame."

She laid her hand friendly on his arm and led him to the window. She sat down on the sill and looked up at him. Blondy stood in awe before her. He yearned to touch her with his fingers.

"What have they done to you? Anything yet?"

"What do you mean?"

"They," she replied waving her hand in the direction of the lower house. "What have they done to you? They treat some pretty mean."

"Nothing . . . yet. They tried once."

"They did? Why didn't you leave?"

"I can't."

"What's the matter?"

"I don't know. I want to, but I can't get away. Your mother won't let me . . . she doesn't hold me," he added quickly. "But I can't leave. I want to get away."

"I'll help you get away tonight," Dorothy promised. "Mother has the same power over you she has over everybody else. Everybody but me. She can't get me. I won't stay here long enough at a time to get caught."

"I want to get away but what will your mother say?"

"Don't talk like that. Don't let Mother get a grip on you because if she does, she will ruin you. You will stay here till you die. Some of them have already."

"Who?"

"The men they brought here." Dorothy stood up beside him and looked in his face. Her head reached only to his shoulders. Blondy wanted to put his arms around her and kiss her. "You know they are all crazy, don't you? All of them. Mother and Poppa and Gertie too. I'd be if I stayed here. I come about once a month to see what's going on and then I leave again as soon as I can. That's what's the matter with Gertie. If she wouldn't come back every time she leaves, she would be all right too. Mother and Poppa are crazy as they can be. It's not safe to stay here. They'll kill you some day."

Blondy sat down weakly on the bed. The revelations of Dorothy made him shiver with fright. He knew there was something queer about the Boxxes. But he could not shake off Mrs. Boxx's influence. Dorothy appeared to be sane and normal. None of the others were, that was a certainty.

For a moment he regained his past strength. He jumped up and threw a chair against the wall. The impact resounded through the house.

"My God! I'm through with this. I'm leaving. I'm going crazy now. I'm going out. I'm going to get away."

He flung open the door and ran past Dorothy down the hall toward the stairway. When he reached the bottom of the stairs, Mrs. Boxx was standing on the last step, blocking his path. She would not let him get away.

When Blondy saw her, he fell into himself and retreated to the second floor. Mrs. Boxx motioned him to come down to her. He went as she told him to do.

"What's the matter with you? Why don't you get to work?"

Blondy apologetically said he would. He went down to the kitchen where she led him. She sat him down on a chair and brought a bucket of potatoes and a knife and told him to peel them.

Turning away she muttered something to herself that was inaudible to Blondy. She called for Jackie and together they went up to her room.

A few minutes later Dorothy came into the kitchen and found Blondy. She went to him and whispered. He shook his head. He was afraid.

"Don't be silly," she whispered. "I'll help you get away tonight when they are asleep. I'll get you out."

She turned and went into the dining room and closed the door behind her. Blondy went to work on the potatoes for Mrs. Boxx.

Boxx, who had been sitting in his accustomed place on the back porch, came into the kitchen and spoke to Blondy. He was polite and talkative.

"Well," he began, "I got a surprise for you. Drop those potatoes a minute and let me show you. Come on."

Blondy got up and followed the man down the cellar steps. Boxx walked in a hurry, taking two steps at a time when he could.

When they were in the cellar, Boxx cautioned Blondy in a half-whisper not to make any noise. He went behind the furnace in the darkness for a small satchel. He blew off the dust and set it down on the burlap bagging in the corner. He sat down beside it and called Blondy to his side.

"Here's something I don't want you to tell anybody about," he began opening the satchel. "It's a secret and I don't want people to know about it. I made it for my own private use."

He opened the satchel and took out a cracked and mildewed leather trousers belt. He took out his handkerchief and wiped the dust and mildew from it carefully. Dangling from the buckle of the belt was a soiled tobacco sack in which there were three marbles. He held the belt up above his head and jingled the marbles in the sack.

"I want to help you," he told Blondy. "I like you a whole lot and I hate to see you get like I used to be before I made this for myself."

Blondy watched Boxx and listened to what he had to say. Boxx required full attention when he talked.

"They," he pointed overhead, "they are going to finish that job on you tonight. I heard my wife and Jackie talking about it. They said they were going to do it this time without fail. Well, I want to help you. Here is what you do: you go up there and let them fix you like they want you. Then you come down here and make you one of these and wear it around your waist like I do when I have use for it. I wouldn't tell you about this, only I hate to see you like I used to be before I made this."

Blondy stared at Boxx and took the tobacco sack in his hand and felt the marbles in it. Boxx stood up and fastened the belt around his waist.

"Look. That's how it works," he stated. "Now you get you one and when you want to fool them and be a man, you'll be as good a one as I am this very minute."

Blondy agreed to do as Boxx advised. This pleased Boxx. He liked to put something over on his wife. He shook Blondy's hand enthusiastically. He tilted back his head and made a gargling sound in his throat.

10

Blondy sat on the edge of his bed waiting to see what was going to happen. He had not seen Dorothy since she left him in the kitchen while he was peeling potatoes for Mrs. Boxx.

Jackie had opened the door once that evening and looked in the room, evidently to make sure that Blondy would be there when Mrs. Boxx was ready for him. Blondy could hear the heavy movements of Mrs. Boxx in the next room. Above all he could hear her sharp squeaky voice when she spoke to Jackie. Jackie's answers were so low he could not hear what he said. Evidently they were making preparations for the operation. Blondy wondered where Dorothy was. He would have searched for her in the house but he was afraid to leave the room. He had been sitting there since supper.

Blondy heard the doctor enter the house on his nightly visit and go upstairs to the third floor. The women talked to him hysterically, begging him to do something to stop the pain they were suffering.

He chuckled to himself and went to another patient and looked at the dressings. He came downstairs after ten minutes and went out. Blondy did not even know his name.

The clock in the hall struck the hour of nine. It was getting late in the house.

Blondy felt helpless without Dorothy. She had promised to help him get away and he was dependent upon her. He could not leave by himself.

Gertie was different. She had brought him there and had done nothing to help him except the time she saved him from Mrs. Boxx's shears. She had gone away again and left him. She would probably come back tonight and help Mrs. Boxx carry out her plan. Gertie was different from Dorothy. Dorothy wanted to help him get away.

At nine-thirty the whole house was still and quiet. There were no lights burning, except the one in Mrs. Boxx's room where she and Jackie were. Blondy sat tensely in the dark listening and hoping Dorothy would come back. She had said she would help him. He knew she would.

Leaning out the window Blondy saw the lights of a truck in the alley behind the house. It stopped at the back gate and two men were walking across the yard to the outside cellar door. Their shadows fell against the high board fence around the back yard. They opened the cellar door and went inside. In a few minutes they reappeared at the door carrying a bundle over their shoulders that looked like a large rolled-up rug. They went across the yard and through the alley gate where the truck stood with its motor running. The driver threw the truck into gear and it rumbled away over the cobblestones. The sound of it died out in the distance. Blondy shut the window and sat down heavily on the bed. It was nearing ten o'clock. Somebody was moving around in Mrs. Boxx's room.

Blondy sat paralyzed on the bed. He was helpless to help himself. He wanted Dorothy to hurry.

Several minutes later Jackie opened the door and switched on the lights. He walked in his catlike stride to the bed and spoke to Blondy.

95

Blondy jumped to his feet trembling all over. Jackie moved toward the door waiting for him to follow. There was nothing else he could do. Mrs. Boxx wanted him and he had to go.

Just as he reached the center of the room, Dorothy ran excitedly in the door. She pushed Jackie back into the room and closed the door behind her, holding it shut by the knob.

"Hurry," she whispered to Blondy. "Put Jackie in the closet and lock the door before Mother hears us."

Blondy grabbed Jackie around his middle and thrust him into the closet. He turned the key in the lock and threw it in the fireplace. Dorothy was waiting to open the door.

He ran to her and jerked open the door with one hand, catching hers with the other. He ran down the hall regardless of the noise they were making. Dorothy was with him. He would not leave without her. He had to have her with him now. At the head of the stairway Mrs. Boxx flung open her door and ran out in the hall.

Before she could see what was happening, Blondy and Dorothy had reached the front door and were running down the steps to the street. Mrs. Boxx ran after them, tumbling down the steps, only to reach the front porch in time to see them disappear around the corner of the block. She realized she was too late to reach them and bring them back to the house. She would only make a disturbance and people would run out in the street asking what the trouble was. She turned defeated and went into her house.

Blondy and Dorothy ran as fast as they could. They had already gone seven or eight blocks since leaving the house and they had no intention of stopping now. They dodged and criss-crossed in the direction of the city. They jumped in the first taxicab they found. It took them to the other side of town, miles away from Mrs. Boxx.

"My God, Dorothy," Blondy squeezed her hand between his, "if it hadn't been for you I'd be there yet, and dead maybe. What's it about your mother that she can make me do anything she wants? This is the first time I've been able to shake her off since Gertie took me there, God only knows how long ago."

"She's crazy, Blondy. But she's got some kind of a power that makes you do anything she wants you to do. That's why I never stay there any longer than I do. If I did stay she would get her grip on me and I'd be like Gertie. Poor Gertie! Gertie's losing her mind by staying there so much. Mother's driving her crazy."

The cab stopped in front of a house and they got out. Dorothy paid the fare.

"Where are we going now?" Blondy asked.

"This is where I live," Dorothy said. "We're going here and rest up a while. You look pretty bad. You look like you've been on a month's drunk, don't you?"

"I'm going to get drunk and stay that way for a month," he said. "I want to try and forget that God damn witch. I know she's your mother, but I can't help hating her like hell."

"I don't blame you," Dorothy said.

They went in the house to a room on the second floor. Blondy was feeling better all the time. And with Dorothy he had never felt better. He liked her.

Dorothy turned on the light and pulled a chair across the room for Blondy. He sat down and stretched his arms and legs pleasurably. It was the first time he had felt this way since he could remember. It seemed to Blondy that he had lived in the Boxx house all his life.

He watched Dorothy take off her hat and put powder on her nose. He wanted to touch her with his fingers and feel her close to him. She made him feel that way about her since the first time he saw her.

He got up and stood beside her. She looked up at him. Her head reached only to his shoulders. He hugged her in his arms.

"You're the sweetest kid I've ever seen," he said to her.

They went to the chair and she sat on his lap and put her arms around his neck. He hugged her tighter and kissed her more and she tightened her arm around his neck.

"You're a peach of a kid," he told her.

She snuggled closer against his chest.

Lord, but he felt good!

PART THREE
DOROTHY

1

Blondy went in the cafe and asked a waiter for Kroot, the proprietor. He sat down at a table and waited.

The midnight crowd was beginning to fill the cafe. Two of the tables were reserved. The electric piano was running full blast playing roll after roll of new jazz. Kroot believed in furnishing his customers with the best and latest in music. He made a lot of money doing that. Otherwise the customers would go where they could hear a lot of good noisy jazz.

Blondy sat and waited for Kroot to come in from the back room where the bar was. It was a quarter of twelve.

Kroot came in and looked at Blondy. He batted his eyes in astonishment.

"What are you doing here?" he asked.

"Never mind that. Sit down," said Blondy kicking back a chair. "I want to ask you something."

"I heard you was . . ." He did not finish.

"Have you seen Salty Banks and Knockout Harris around here lately?"

"Sure. They come in here about every night around this time. Do you want to see them? They told me you . . ."

"That's all I want to know now. I just wanted to know where I could find them. I've got a little bill to collect."

"Look here," Kroot said edging his chair closer to Blondy. "You're not going to start anything here, are you? You'll have to get out if you do. Every time there's a fight in here I lose money. The customers would a lot rather see a fight than eat any time."

"There won't be no fight. I'm just going to collect a little bill. That's all."

"All right. But I'm telling you. If you start anything . . . out you go."

"Bring me something to eat. I'm waiting for Salty Banks."

Kroot called a waiter to the table. The waiter took Blondy's order while Kroot went back to the bar. He got his gun and buckled it on. He was not taking any chances with Blondy Niles around.

Blondy sat back in his chair with his eyes on the door. If Salty and Knockout did come in tonight he was going to be the first to know about it. The waiter brought his food.

Kroot came in and sat down at the table with Blondy again. Blondy glanced up at him and continued eating.

"Let me give you a little advice," Kroot said in a whisper. "I'm telling you something that's good for you."

"What's it about?"

"You aint got a chance by yourself. Why don't you get a gang together? You can't do nothing alone these days. You got to have a bunch to get anywhere."

"Listen. I just want to collect a little debt owing to me. That's all. Salty Banks owes me some money and I'm going to collect it. That's all."

"Well, I'm just telling you too. You can't get nowhere these days by yourself. You'll have a hell of a time getting money out of Salty Banks by yourself if he don't want to give it to you. But if you had a bunch, well . . . well, you'd get it all right and get it quick. That's the way it is now. I know all about it. I used to be like you are about it, but I found out you got to have a bunch to get anywhere. I know."

"I'll get the money," Blondy said. "And I won't mess up your joint either."

"Look!" Kroot whispered behind his hand and nodding his head toward the door. "There they are now."

Salty and Knockout came in with a girl between them. Salty looked around the room for a table. He did not seen Blondy. The girl evidently belonged to Knockout. She hung to his arm and gave no attention to Salty. It was costing Knockout a barrel of money to keep her too, because he was black.

Blondy stood up and called Salty. Salty looked across the room surprised at seeing Blondy. He caught Knockout's arm and pointed across the room at Blondy. Neither had anything to say. For a moment they seemed to be trying to decide whether to stay or leave the cafe. Blondy sent Kroot after them.

They came up to the table.

"Sit down," Blondy said opening his mouth enough to make the words audible. "All of you sit down."

The girl with Knockout was frisky. She tried to soften Blondy's scowl with her eyes.

"What's the matter with the kid? Is he mad at you?" she asked Salty.

"Shut up and sit down," Blondy said.

The three of them sat down. The girl's chair was so close to Blondy's elbow she touched him.

"Well, how about it?" he asked Salty.

Both Salty and Knockout knew what he was talking about. Salty pretended he did not know.

"How about what?"

"Quit your stalling. You know what I want. I want the ten grand in heavy lumps and I want it now. I'm tired of waiting for it. What about it?"

"Say, Blondy, I aint collected yet," Salty lied. "I been trying to collect for all of us nearly two months now. When I get it you'll get yours the first thing. I'll see to that."

"You're a God damn liar, you are. You already got it and I want mine. I'm ready to collect now. What about it? Yes or no?"

Kroot stood against the wall with two of his biggest waiters beside him. Each of them had a blunt-nosed shot gun pushed under his coat. Kroot was not taking any chances. He had to protect his trade.

The girl tried to put her arm around Blondy's neck, but he shook her off. Salty had put her up to it to keep Blondy quiet. She did her best to quiet him.

"I'm waiting," Blondy said in low even voice.

The crowd in the cafe was waiting for something to happen. The people nearest the table had got up and moved toward the door where they could get out in the street quickly if anything started. Everybody wanted to see something happen.

"Listen," Salty begged, cornered, "I'll get you yours tomorrow and meet you tomorrow night and give it to you if you're so damn set on having it. Me and Knockout have got to wait on ours, why can't you wait too?"

"To hell with that waiting stuff. I'm getting mine now. I'll give you twenty-four hours to get it. And you'd better have it too, by God. Ten thousand. No more and no less. And if you don't get it to me I'll have to take it out myself. But that'd make a pretty expensive funeral for a man like you, Salty. A corpse costing ten grand is pretty expensive. Aint it, Salty?"

Knockout had not said a word since they came in. He was afraid of Blondy. He was playing safe.

"Come on, let's go," Salty said to the girl and Knockout.

"I'm giving you plenty of warning," Blondy said. "I'm going to have it by this time tomorrow, or else . . ."

"Come on," Salty urged them.

"Wait a minute. Where you going to meet me tomorrow night?"

"On the corner below," Salty promised. "On the corner at eleven sharp. I'll be there with it."

Blondy sat down and watched them go through the door. Salty was mad and Knockout was scared. Salty was a dangerous man to deal with. He would do anything to keep from paying out money.

Kroot came over to the table as soon as they had gone. He was mad about what had happened.

"I thought I told you not to start anything?"

"Hell, what do you want? I didn't pull no gun. What's wrong with you?"

"You made him mad. He's liable to come back any minute and shoot the whole place up. And you made them leave before they bought anything. They was going to spend money for three suppers."

"Salty Banks aint going to shoot nothing up when I'm around. I can handle Salty with no trouble at all."

"You'll have to get out anyway. I can't take no chances. He might come back with a gang."

"Listen," Blondy said. "I'm leaving right now but not because you want me to leave. I'm going because I'm ready to go. See? What you got upstairs now? Anything?"

"Why don't you go up and see? There's always something up there."

"That's what I'm going to do. But I'm just going to look around. I don't want nothing you've got up there or ever will have. I'm fixed all right myself somewhere else now."

"Go on up. You might find something you like up there."

Blondy pushed back his chair and threw a silver dollar on the table.

"Give me fifty cents change."

Kroot gave him fifty cents change without a moment's hesitation. Actually the bill the waiter had made out amounted to eighty-five cents.

Blondy put the money in his pocket and pushed by Kroot. Kroot gladly stepped out of Blondy's way. He wanted to get Blondy out of the cafe as quickly as possible. Salty might come back any second now.

2

Blondy climbed the stairs and felt his way along the hall. A dim light at the further end was the only illumination. He chose one of the doors at random. It was locked. He tried another.

He opened the second door and threw it forward. It banged against the wall inside. The girl sat on the bed wearing a red kimono. She held a mirror in her hand looking at her face. Blondy took a second look at her and went to another room.

Going to the last room on the hall he opened the door and walked in. The girl was standing with her back to the door looking out the window. She turned around when he made the noise of entering.

"Hello," she said.

She looked all right. Much better than the woman who got mad because he left her up the hall.

"I know who you are," she said coming to him in the center of the room.

"Who am I?"

"You're Blondy Niles."

"That's right. And what about it?"

"You're the one Louise was crazy about. She used to tell me all about you. She sure was crazy about you."

"You knew Louise?" Blondy asked shaking her arm. "Did you know her?"

"Sure I did. We were always going around together before she got killed. Say, why don't they do something to Salty Banks for killing her?"

"Who?"

"Salty Banks."

"How do you know Salty killed her? Who told you that?"

"Salty didn't exactly kill her himself. He had two killers do it for him. I know all about it."

"Listen here: are you lying to me? Did Salty Banks have anything to do with it?"

"Honest to God! Salty said she was too wise. He said he didn't want her around when he was trying to frame you for the fights with Knockout."

"Say," Blondy demanded shaking her roughly by the shoulders. "Who told you all this?"

"His name was Big John something or other. He was one of the killers who did it for Salty. He was drunk when he told me. He wouldn't have told me if he had known what he was saying. Salty would push him off if he knew about it."

Blondy grabbed her shoulders and shook her violently. He choked her with his fingers.

"Are you telling me the truth? I'll choke you off if you're lying about it."

"Honest to God!" she struggled with her breath. "Let me loose and I'll tell you all I know about it. Louise was my friend. I hated to see her get pushed off like that. I wish they'd sit Salty Banks on the hot-seat for it."

Blondy sat down on the bed in a daze. He was trying to figure out a way to fix Salty. He wished he could choke him to death a dozen times for what he had done to Louise.

"Salty paid the two killers a hundred dollars apiece to push her off," the girl said. She sat down beside him on the bed. "They pushed her off while you were at a roadhouse somewhere."

Blondy got up giving the girl a five dollar bill and went downstairs.

He went home to Dorothy and went to bed thinking about what he was going to do to Salty Banks. Dorothy had fallen to sleep waiting for him. He did not wake her.

3

The early afternoon sun falling on the bed moved slowly towards Blondy's face. When the beams reached his eyes he opened them and blinked sleepily at the glare. He turned his face away from the light. It was twelve o'clock by the clock on the table.

Blondy sat up in bed and looked at Dorothy sleeping soundly two feet away in the other bed. She had waited up for him until she fell asleep just before he came in at one-thirty.

He looked at her slightly parted lips undecided whether to kiss them. He liked Dorothy. He thought she was going to be straight with him. But Louise was on his mind. He could never get over the loss of her. If she had lived he would be with her now. He would not be undecided about kissing her. He would have kissed her as soon as he waked up. But Dorothy was all right. He would like her more and more as they lived together. But he would never forget Louise. He had loved her too much to forget easily.

While he was sitting on the side of his bed looking at her she opened her eyes and saw him. She smiled and stretched her arms above her head.

"Hello, darling. Where did you go last night? I must have fallen asleep waiting for you."

He liked the way she called him darling. It sounded like it really meant something the way she said it every time.

He tossed aside the cover and sat down on the side of her bed, supporting himself with his stiffened arm on the other side of her. She reached for his other hand and kissed it solemnly.

"Dorothy, I'm going to kill Salty Banks tonight."

"What!"

She sat erectly up in bed pushing back the hair from her forehead and looking wildly at him. She caught his hand and pulled at him excitedly.

"What?" she repeated.

"I'm going to kill Salty."

She threw her arms around his neck and shook him.

"Darling, don't do that! They will get you and kill you too!"

"He had Louise killed."

"My God! He did! How do you know?"

"I heard last night. I'm going to fix him for it all right."

"Darling, don't do that. Please don't. They'll get you sure. You can't get away with it."

"I don't care what happens to me if I get him."

"But darling, let them get Salty. They'll fix him. All you have to do is tell them and they'll fix him. And then you won't get into trouble."

"Have you got a good gun?"

"Please, darling, don't do that! I'll go and tell the police myself that Salty did it. Won't you let me tell them?"

"I've made up my mind to do it and I'm going to get Salty myself. I've got to get a good gun somewhere. One that will fix him so he'll stay fixed."

"Let me do it then, darling. They'll send you to the chair sure. Let me do it, darling, please. I can do it just as good as you can."

"I'm going to do it myself tonight. I've got to find a good gun somewhere now."

Blondy got up from the bed and began dressing hurriedly. Dorothy jumped up and threw her arms around his neck begging him not to get into trouble.

Pushing her away he finished dressing. Dorothy dressed as quickly as she could. Blondy waited for her, sitting in the window smoking cigarettes. When she was ready to go she came over to him and begged him not to kill Salty. She did not want him to be sentenced for murder. And they would surely get him if he killed Salty. They knew he had been having trouble about the money Salty owed him. Blondy would not listen to her.

Dorothy pleaded with him all the way to the restaurant where they went for breakfast. Blondy had made up his mind. She wiped the tears from her face and went inside with him.

"Please darling," she begged. "Please don't do anything like that. Let Salty alone. We'll take a trip and have a good time and forget all about it. We'll have a lot of fun together, darling."

"Listen, Dorothy," Blondy said. "Salty had Louise murdered. I was going to marry her with the money I made out of the two fights with Knockout. Salty didn't want Louise around to help collect the money, so he had her killed. He won't even give me the money now."

"Don't get like that, darling."

"I saw him last night and I told him I was going to have the money tonight and he said he'd produce it. Well, he's going to meet me tonight and give it to me. When he gets there I'm going to finish him. That's all."

"Who told you Salty had her killed?"

"A girl at the cafe."

"She might have been lying to you, darling. How do you know she was telling the truth?"

"She was one of Louise's pals. Somebody told her about it and

112

she told me. She knew I had taken up with Louise. She told me all about it. She was telling the truth. Salty did it."

"Darling, let's get somebody else to do it then," she suggested hopefully.

"I want to do it myself. I want to see the bastard when he dies."

"Somebody else could do it just as good as you can. Couldn't they, darling?"

"I want to see him die. I want to see him when he falls down and can't get up again . . . the son of a bitch."

"But darling, you'll be sent to the chair for that. Don't you know you will?"

"I don't care, I'm no good anyway. What in hell am I good for? Nothing. I started out fighting and got soaked and had to quit because nobody would give me a fight. All they ever wanted was me to let the other fighter win so they could take in a lot of bets. I'm no damn good. What's the use of being nothing? I'd rather get pushed off myself than let somebody else get Salty for me. I'll be satisfied if I get Salty Banks."

"Sure you are good, darling. You've never had a chance to get anywhere. You always tied up with men like Salty Banks and they don't give a damn about you. If you had somebody to look out for you and tell the others how and when to go to hell you'd come on top."

"Nobody's going to take me up now. They think I quit every time I start."

"I could help a lot, darling."

"How?"

"Helping you get the right fights and collecting when it's due you."

"No, you couldn't. Louise tried that and Salty put a stop to it. He won't let nobody butt in with him. He'd push you off too if you got mixed up in my fights."

"You don't have to fight for Salty Banks always. There are other men who would get you fights and look after you."

"Where in hell are they? Nobody's going to take me up now. Nobody."

"Darling, please don't get into trouble about Salty. He's not worth getting sent to the chair for."

"I don't give a damn about him. It's Louise. I'm getting him for pushing Louise off. That's all. I don't give a damn about Salty Banks. I'm just going to put some lead and steel in him for that. That's all I care about."

"Well, darling, if you are going to do it and won't listen to me, I'll help you. What do you want me to do, darling?"

"Listen, Dorothy, you go out and get the gun for me, will you? You do that and I'll do the rest. Get a good one. Six shooter. A thirty-eight will be about right for him. And get a dozen steel bullets for it. I'll wait at home for you."

"All right, darling. I'll do it. I'll do anything in the world you want me to do."

"I'll wait for you, Dorothy. You get the gun and I'll do the rest. And, by God, I'm going to do a damn good job, too!"

"I'll be home as soon as I can, darling."

"You're a good kid, Dorothy," he said.

4

Mrs. Boxx stepped silently in her felt bedroom slippers from the third floor to the cellar and back again. She had Jackie to help her with the women on the top floor when she had to go up there, and the rest of the time she played with him in her bedroom. Gertie had promised to bring home a man the night before but she came back alone. Tonight she had gone into town again in search of somebody who could be made to take the place of Blondy in the house.

Upstairs the patients lay awake suffering and waiting for the doctor to come. He would do nothing to relieve their pain when he did come, but they always looked forward with the hope that he would this time. It was past the hour when he was due and most of them had almost given up hope of seeing him until the next day. The suffering they had to endure because of lack of attention was enough in itself to cause death. Anyway, it hastened it. Mrs. Boxx was their nurse and it was her duty to help them when the physician was not there.

Mrs. Boxx however was more intent on finding new bodies to carry to the cellar and on admitting new patients to the house than she was with anything that would help them to get well, or even to live longer. The linen on most of the beds had not been changed in several weeks. When one side of the sheet became too dirty she turned it over. This continued, this turning and returning of linen, until it was so dirty it soiled the bodies of the patients. Usually each sheet and pillow case lasted a month.

Mrs. Boxx went to her room and played with Jackie, listening for Gertie and hoping she would bring home a man when she came. Jackie was all right. But what she wanted now was a new man. Jackie was all right when there was nobody else.

"Come here, Jackie. Sit on my lap," she told him.

Jackie sat himself on her short fat legs and leaned back against the breasts that hung like a couple of half-filled hot-water bags from her chest.

"What do you want to do now, dear Mrs. Boxx?" he asked, resting comfortably against her mountainous body.

"I'm going to tickle you, Jackie!"

Saturday night was always the biggest one of the week at the roadhouse of which Salty's friend, Jocas, was the sole owner and one manager. On Saturday nights everybody went upstairs and joined in a dance. It was called a costume dance. The men put on aprons and rubber boots; the girls undressed and put on even less. Then the music began and everybody got out and danced. The intermission came at midnight.

After everybody had gone downstairs to the bar and had several good drinks and walked around for ten or fifteen minutes they came back upstairs for the show. The show was a dance by the girls at the end of the hall. The men went to the other end waiting until the dance began. When the orchestra started playing the men moved slowly across the hall until they reached the girls. Then each man selected the girl he would like to have and walked in and took her. When two or more men chose the same girl, which happened right and left, the big fight started.

The fights were the high spots of a big night. The men who opened the fight soon became secondary to it. Everybody joined and participated with enthusiasm. It began with quick well-directed uppercuts and jaw-crunchers and ended in everybody being beaten up until nobody could hit hard enough to hurt even one of the girls. When this stage was reached, the lights were turned on and the waiters served double-decked drinks on the house.

The rooms on the top floor of the warehouse in which Louise and Blondy had lived, had been let to two girls who wanted to live up there. It was a convenient location.

The street on which the building faced was one leading up from the river to the cafes and lodging houses. And the street on the other side was well filled with stores that were open until midnight, and with cafes and hotels.

The girls who rented the rooms made their living by bringing men up there from the street. They went down and walked up and down the streets until two men came along who were looking for two girls like them. The girls were nice looking, and men were fairly easy to get. There were two beds in the rooms now, and they had a small oil stove on which they cooked breakfast and dinner. They ate supper every night in one of the cafes along the street, because there were always men there who came over to the table and talked to them. When they were ready to go, the men paid their checks and went home with them.

The cafe began filling up at eleven o'clock, and from then until daylight it was crowded. Men came in after their early evening jobs were done and brought their women with them for some fun and something to eat, or else they came there and found plenty of women at the tables. The men who came there were those who lived hard. They were part of the underworld that had its outcropping down here near the river.

5

Salty Banks put Knockout and the girl out of the taxi and went down to a hotel on Meldon Street near the waterfront. The hotel was patronized by rivermen and those men who wanted a place where they could go and talk things over quietly. It was quiet down there at night and the street lamps were dim.

Salty hired a room and called up two men he knew. They answered the phone immediately. They could come over right away. Salty sent for some drinks and waited for the men to come.

It was between one and two o'clock.

Big John and Roughhead came in the room ten minutes after Salty called them. They took some drinks from the bottle. They were breezy and talkative. Salty sat in the chair thinking hard for five minutes before speaking to them. They did not mind waiting. The bottle was for them.

Big John and Roughhead were short and thickly made. Their

shoulders were wide and their hips deep. Their legs were short and bulging. Neither of them wore a collar on their shirts. When they bought a new shirt they ripped off the collar. Collars were uncomfortable around their short necks.

"I've got another job to do," Salty explained after several minutes.

"Right," said Roughhead. "Right."

"Listen," said Salty handing them an unopened bottle. "There's this bastard named Blondy Niles, who wants to collect some money from me. I'm not coming across. See? What I want you to do is to quiet him and make him stay quiet. See?"

"Push him all the way off?" Big John wanted to know. He asked that because it meant double the money. If they were only to beat him up they would get just half as much.

"Sure all the way, so he can't come back."

"Right," said Roughhead. "Put some flowers in his hand, eh?"

"Flowers and plenty of them," insisted Salty. "He won't have no more birthdays."

"Right," said Roughhead. "Right."

"How much this time?" Big John asked. "Same lump?"

"A lump apiece," Salty promised.

"Right," Roughhead said. "Right."

"A hundred when?" Big John wanted to know.

"On the spot. Just like it was last time."

"Right."

"I'll meet you here at ten sharp tomorrow night and we'll pull it off at eleven sharp. He's to meet me at a place then."

"Right," said Roughhead. "Ten sharp. We'll be here waiting."

Salty opened the door and let them out. He went back and opened up a fresh bottle for himself.

The electric piano started early and played almost continuously until six in the morning. Usually it was shut down for half an hour, beginning at two o'clock, to allow the parts to cool. Then it was that some of the men went upstairs to see the girls up there. If they had women with them they sometimes took them upstairs, other times telling them to wait until they came back. The girls upstairs waited all night.

Kroot, the owner of the cafe, was making a lot of money. Much more money than he had made when he was a weight-lifter in the circus, or even when he ran a saloon. Here in the cafe he made twice as much as he had ever made before. The cafe was known to everybody on the waterfront and everybody came there sometime during the night. Once for several weeks he had experimented with having girls for waiters, but he gave that up quickly and hired men for the jobs again. All too frequently a customer came in and picked up one of the waitresses in his arms and carried her home with him. Kroot had to switch back to men. He had the girls go upstairs for his rooms.

Salty went up to his room in the hotel and sat down to wait for Big John and Roughhead. They were due in ten minutes.

Salty sat in the chair swearing at Blondy. He was afraid of him. He might find out how Louise was killed and do something about it. Salty was anxious to get him out of the way as soon as possible. For the sooner he was dead the safer his own life would be. Blondy was dangerous when he was angry. He was still mad about the way the last fight turned out. He might even try to do something about that too. Salty cursed him and looked at his watch.

Big John and Roughhead knocked on the door and came in immediately. They were ready for their work. Their collars were turned up hiding their shirts and their hips bulged with revolvers. Roughhead carried the machine gun under his coat.

"All right," Salty said nervously. "You're on time. Everything all right?"

Roughhead took the machine gun from under his coat and laid it on the table.

"Right," he said. "She's working like a nigger full of turpentine tonight. We tried her out to make sure. She's slick."

"Right," Big John said. "Everything's right."

"Come here," Salty said motioning them beside him on the bed. "Now look here: Here's the layout. This is how it's going to work."

121

"Right," said Roughhead. "Let's have it."

"We'll cruise around down at this place near the cafe for ten or fifteen minutes, getting the come-and-go straight. See? At eleven sharp this Blondy bastard is going to be standing on the corner below the cafe waiting for me to hand over some lumps to him. He might have a rod, so we won't take no chances with that. We'll get in the ride and roll down the street past the corner about ten minutes to eleven and go down to the end of the street at the dock and wait a few minutes. That will give us plenty of time to get started up the street so as to get on the corner at eleven. He'll be waiting. But if he's not, we'll go up the street and roll back and do it again. We might have to do it three times, but the chances are we'll get him the first one."

"Right," Roughhead said. "Right."

"Well then. Now here is where you birds come in . . . say, which of you pulls the trigger?"

"I'm the doctor," Roughhead said. "Big John is the nurse."

"All right. You got the layout. Now when we spot him on the corner, then is when you do the job. Big John will work the door for you and steady your aim. We'll shove the ride into second so he can have plenty of power for a quick start, and it will slow us down enough to get a good target too."

"Right," Big John said. "Right."

"Now, Roughhead, you plug away at him till he drops and keep it up as long as you've got a target. See? If he drops the first time, pump away till it's pumped out. Hop those pills in him till he falls apart. We aint taking no chances. We want to do the job right the first time and it will all be over."

Roughhead took out his handkerchief and polished the machine gun until the blue steel glistened in the light. It had already had a lot of usage. Roughhead took good care of it.

"Now," Salty asked, "is everything straight? Now's the time to get it right."

"Right," said Big John. "Right."

"There's one thing more. This Blondy might switch corners on us.

He might be standing on any of the four. What we'll do will be to spot that when we roll down to the river. We'll be ready to use both sides of the ride. Big John you're working the doors."

"Right," he said. "Right."

Salty took out his watch and looked at the time. It was ten-thirty. It was time to get started. They had twenty blocks to go before they reached the dock at the end of the street.

Roughhead picked up the machine gun and lifted it under his coat. He handled it more carefully than he would a baby.

Big John switched off the lights and they went out of the hotel.

6

Dorothy went to the door with Blondy. She drew his head down against her breast and kissed him a dozen or more times.

"Please, darling, be careful," she begged, pulling at him desperately. "Please don't let them get you."

"I'm all right. I'll be back in an hour. It won't take me long to fix Salty. I wish Knockout Harris was going to be there too. Maybe he will. I'd like to fix him at the same time."

"Please don't let him get you, darling. You won't, will you?"

"Listen, Dorothy, I'm going after Salty. He's the one that's going to get it. I'll be back in an hour. Just wait and see if I don't."

"I'm going to wait right here by the door till you come back, darling. I'm not going to move an inch till you come back."

Blondy opened the door and paused in the doorway.

"If I'm not back in about two hours don't wait up for me," he said closing the door behind him.

Dorothy sat down in a chair and waited for Blondy to come back. She had wanted to go along to take care of him in case anything did happen, but he made her stay there. She held the clock in her two hands, and looked at it.

Blondy ran out on the street and found a taxi. He took out his watch and studied the hands and numerals for a minute or longer. Then he jumped in the cab and rode away after Salty Banks.

Blondy reached the place he wanted to leave the cab at fifteen minutes to eleven. He was a block away from the corner where he was to meet Salty. Salty said he would be there at eleven sharp. It was fifteen minutes until he was due.

Blondy walked around the block and emerged on the street on which stood the building where he had lived with Louise. There was the corner at which he was to meet Salty. He walked past the building on the opposite side of the street studying the position he planned to take. Salty would probably come down the street on which he now stood, or else east on the other street running parallel with the river. In either case he would be able to see Salty before Salty saw him. There was an electric light pole on the corner and beside it a large mail box, big enough to conceal the figure of a man. Blondy stooped down beside it and began laying his trap for Salty.

Salty would probably come down the street toward the river and cross the square to the opposite corner. When he was in the centre of the square, Blondy would target him. Nothing would work better. He went back to the wall of the building and waited for his watch to tell him it was time to get ready for Salty. It was seven minutes to eleven now.

An automobile sped down the street toward the river. Blondy kept his eyes on the car and looked up the street for Salty. It was nearing the time when he should arrive. While he was watching the street ahead the automobile came back up the street from the dock. It was the same car that had gone down only a few minutes before. It had turned around at the dock.

Blondy glanced hastily at the watch and went over behind the

125

mail box beside the electric light pole. It was three minutes to eleven. Salty would be there any second now. He said eleven sharp. It was close to it.

Two men came west on the cross street and went through the square without noticing Blondy. They were going toward the cafe in the middle of the next block.

The automobile that was coming up the street from the river had slowed down and was moving slowly in second gear at about ten miles an hour. Blondy watched the street for Salty Banks.

When the automobile was nearly in the square, the rear door sprang open and the barrel of a gun began spitting fire and lead at him. As soon as he heard the first sound of the gun he ducked behind the steel mail box, but he was too late. Two of the bullets had hit him in the chest. The others coming as close behind each other as beads on a string, hit against the mail box. They were being fired from an angle now and the bullets glanced off the steel toward the river. Almost before he knew what had happened, the car was gone and everything was quiet and still.

Blondy sank on his knees beside the mail box and felt the wounds in his left chest. The bullets had torn oblong holes in his body and lodged somewhere inside of him. The blood was flowing freely.

Blondy got to his feet and staggered across the street, falling against the wall of the building. He was getting weak from the loss of blood.

He started toward the entrance to the building. Before he had gone a dozen paces he fell to the pavement. His coat and shirt were wet with blood. He got on his knees and crawled along the street close to the wall, leaning against it for support. He reached the door and opened it. He did not know where he was going, except that he knew he had once lived there with Louise.

Long before he reached the top floor he had become so weak he could move only by pushing and pulling himself over the edges of the steps. His knees and elbows bent under him.

Semi-conscious he found the door and lay against it. It was several minutes before he had the strength to knock his head against it. Almost immediately the door opened and he fell inside on his back. The two girls shrieked at what they saw. They ran back into the room huddling against the wall.

"My God, look at that man!" one of them exclaimed.

The other girl screamed when he tried to get up and fell on his face.

The girl who had spoken went over to Blondy and turned his face up and looked at it.

"Do you know him?" she asked the other girl.

"I never saw him before."

"He must be dying . . . look at him. Look how he's bleeding."

Together they lifted and dragged him into the room and lay him on the floor. They were trying to decide what they should do with him when Blondy opened his eyes. He saw the girl nearest him.

"Louise," he murmured almost inaudibly. "Louise . . ."

Neither of the girls could understand what he said. They looked at each other frightened.

"Louise," he murmured again. His strength was leaving him.

He attempted to raise his hand toward the girl, but it fell limply on the floor beside him.

The two girls huddled together, wondering what to do. They saw he was dying fast.

Once more Blondy opened his eyes and looked up at the girl. He struggled with the tongue in his throat.

"Louise . . . I tried to . . . get . . ." He never finished what he wanted to say.

The two girls were so frightened they could not run for help. They were afraid to move from the room. One of them closed the door and the other bent over him to make certain he was not alive. There was no heartbeat and the breath was still.

They went to the window and whispered to each other cautiously, as though they were afraid he would hear them. They came back to the body and lifted it across the room to the window. They struggled with the heavy weight but managed to lift it to the sill. With it there they were able to push it out into the night. Leaning out listening for it to strike the water they waited for what seemed like an hour before it splashed into the river below the window. That was all. There was no more sound.

"Who was he?" the younger girl asked.

"I don't know. I never saw him before in my life."

"Well, he had a hell of a nerve coming here to die. Why couldn't he have gone home and done it?"

"The poor fool probably didn't have a home," the other said.

7

Dorothy waited by the door, clock in hand, for three long hours. It was nearly half past two. Blondy told her he would get back in an hour. He was two hours late.

Dorothy threw the clock across the room and, snatching up hat and coat, ran out to the street. She ran all the way to the corner where Blondy went to meet Salty at eleven o'clock.

She ran up the street and down it, across the square and back again. Nobody was in sight. Nobody to ask if anything had happened to Blondy. Blondy was not there, nor was Salty. Under the street lamp she found the pool of blood Blondy had left on the pavement beside the mail box. She fell on her hands and knees and rubbed her fingers in it. It was wet.

Crawling she followed the trail of blood on her hands and knees across the street and down to the door of the building. The door was smeared with it, as if his hand bled.

Fumbling for her cigarette lighter she followed the trail up over the stairway. She ran, half stooping, following it to the last floor of the building. Again it stopped in front of a door, and the door was smeared with the blood.

Dorothy burst open the door and ran inside the room, holding the thin flame of light over her head to guide her.

The girl in the room cried out in fright. She had been awakened by Dorothy's scream when she found more blood on the floor. She sat up in bed holding the blankets around her protectingly.

"Who is that?" the girl cried out.

Dorothy lit the lamp on the table and looked at the girl. Dorothy was trembling. The other was frightened too.

"Where is he?" Dorothy shouted, running to the girl and shaking her.

The girl in the next room ran in, awakened by the noise Dorothy was making. She had a revolver in her hand. She too trembled.

"What do you want?" she asked.

"Where is he?" Dorothy screamed. "Where is he?"

Neither of the girls answered her. They were afraid of her.

"Where is he?" she pleaded. "What did you do with him? Where is he now?"

The girl with the pistol came to the bed and sat down.

"The man who was shot?" she asked.

"Yes! Blondy! Where is he?"

The girl in the bed drew the blankets around her shoulders. The wind that blew through the window was cold and damp.

"You've got a hell of a nerve coming here and waking us up. What do you want?"

"Blondy! Where is he? Tell me! Where is he?"

"A man came in here a couple of hours ago and fell out the window, if that's who you mean. He was shot up."

"Oh my God! Blondy!" Dorothy screamed, throwing herself against the window trying to see below in the darkness.

The two girls huddled together on the bed watching Dorothy. The night air was cold and damp.

Dorothy ran to them from the window.

"Is he dead?"

"Why shouldn't he be? He was shot up. He didn't live long. He had holes in his chest. He's fifty feet under water now anyway. Sure he's dead now."

Dorothy ran back to the window and leaned out trying to see what was in the dark below. The only sound was the swishing of water against the side of the building. All else was dark and still.

The girls looked at each other wondering when Dorothy would go away and let them go to sleep. They wanted to go back to bed.

When they turned around and looked again, Dorothy was not in the room. She had jumped into the river. They heard the splash of her body and then there was no more sound from her. The girl with the revolver stood up and looked at the other girl.

"Now what do you know about that!" she said.

"The poor fool didn't have any better sense, if you ask me."

"Poor fool?" the other said derisively, going back to her room. "You mean the damn fool. She was a damn fool. The man she called Blondy was the poor fool. He couldn't help himself."

$\mathcal{V}$OICES OF THE $\mathcal{S}$OUTH

Erskine Caldwell, *Poor Fool*

Fred Chappell, *The Gaudy Place*

Ellen Douglas, *The Rock Cried Out*

George Garrett, *Do, Lord, Remember Me*

Willie Morris, *The Last of the Southern Girls*

Lee Smith, *The Last Day the Dogbushes Bloomed*

Elizabeth Spencer, *The Voice at the Back Door*

Peter Taylor, *The Widows of Thornton*

Robert Penn Warren, *Band of Angels*

Joan Williams, *The Morning and the Evening*